ILY'S LOST SOLDIER

ASHLEY WHITNEY

First published in 2025 by Vignette House

Published in the United States of America

ISBN 978-1-988557-68-7 (Paperback)
ISBN 978-1-988557-69-4 (Hardcover)
ISBN 978-1-988557-67-0 (E-book)

Library of Congress Control Number: 2025939050

*To my grandparents
and great-grandparents*

Dear Momma,

The South is gaining more and more control over us every day. We're practically on our knees over here. Soon the North is going to be defeated. No one knows who's from which side anymore; we're all mixed in with the enemy now! We also have a spy amongst us, but Momma, don't worry--I'm coming home!

Love, Billy

TABLE OF CONTENTS

1

ILY

The weather was fine when Ily received the letter that would send her husband away. The dust storms had finally passed, and it was the first sunny day in a week. The air was beginning to warm again, a sure sign that spring was just around the corner. Thomas was outside, surveying the damage to his field and wondering whether he would be able to plant this year. Meanwhile, Ily had just finished sweeping away the last bit of dust that had managed to creep through the cracks in the doors and windows.

Ily stepped out onto the front porch, brushing aside the auburn strands that had escaped from the handkerchief tied around her hair. She dusted off her worn, faded cleaning rags and gazed at the small patch of land in front of her. Despite everything, she had never felt prouder.

Ily and Thomas's cornfield stretched up a hill to the right of their modest single-story, two-bedroom house, while the barn and chicken coop—connected to the side of the barn—stood to the left. The chicken wire seemed to be holding steady after a recent repair. The foxes had struck again not long ago, ripping a hole in the wire and making off with three chickens and two dozen eggs. Now, only two hens remained.

Ily turned toward the field to call Thomas in for lunch, but before she could, she caught sight of Mr. Kay walking up the dirt-and-gravel road leading to their house.

Mr. Kay delivered mail in Keyes, Oklahoma, a small panhandle town with a population of about 250, located roughly 20 miles from Boise City. There was only one main road leading in and out of town, with another branch connecting to the homes of Ily and Thomas Milton, Betsy and Eddie Ryeson, and a few others.

The road to Keyes passed a small cemetery and led to the center of town, where a windmill stood proudly in front of the courthouse and bank. Lining the main street were the one-room schoolhouse, the blacksmith, the post office beside the barbershop, and the mercantile across from the doctor's office. Toward the edge of town, the towering newspaper building seemed to loom over the nearby homes, as if spying on the townsfolk.

Mr. Kay smoothed back his short gray hair and wiped the sweat from his brow before replacing his cap. As he approached, he waved to Ily with a warm smile.

"How are you, Mrs. Milton?" he asked.

Mr. Kay was well-liked by everyone in town, but preferred the formality of last names, a habit instilled by his strict upbringing. Since losing his wife to dust pneumonia two years earlier, he had devoted himself entirely to his job. Delivering mail and chatting with the townspeople brought him comfort.

"Fine, thank you," Ily replied with a smile. "And you?"

"Just fine. Beautiful day we're having. Better enjoy it while it lasts."

"I know what you mean. Thomas has been out in the fields all morning. I was just about to call him in for some lunch. Would you like some stew before heading back to town?"

"Oh, no, that's quite alright. I still have a few more letters to deliver. I thank you, though. Please tell Mr. Milton I said hello."

Mr. Kay handed Ily a letter and tipped his cap before heading back down the road. Ily waved goodbye and turned toward the field, climbing the hill to find Thomas.

"Mail came today," Ily said as Thomas soaked up the last of his stew with a piece of bread and drained his glass of milk.

"Oh? What'd we get?" Thomas asked.

His hair, normally dark and thick, had been lightened by a coating of dust, and even after washing, his deeply tanned skin appeared pale.

Ily stood and retrieved the letter from the counter. Her breath caught as she recognized the government seal stamped on the envelope and the formal typed print of the address.

```
From: U.S. Army Corps
To: Mr. Thomas Milton
         URGENT
```

Ily knew this could only mean one thing. She handed Thomas the official envelope, then headed to her red floral-printed chair in the sitting room while Thomas opened and read the letter.

```
                         February 5th, 1935

Dear Mr. Milton,

We have encountered setbacks at the front
in North Carolina and urgently require
your assistance to regain control of South
Carolina. You are instructed to report to
the local post office in Boise City on March
15th, where transportation to boot camp
will be provided. Training will commence
on March 18th and conclude on May 8th.
Upon completing your training, you will
be stationed at the base camp in Monroe,
North Carolina. When not deployed at the
front lines, you will remain at the camp.

Your country deeply values your service
and extends its gratitude and honor for
your commitment.

                  United States Army Corps
```

Thomas jumped out of his chair and rushed over to Ily.

"Ily, they need me. They need me over in North Carolina!" he exclaimed.

Ily stared at her husband of seven years with wide eyes.

"This is good for us," Thomas insisted.

"How can war be good for us?" Ily nearly shouted.

But she knew that Thomas had always dreamed of joining the Army, always willing to lend a helping hand.

The war between North and South Carolina had been dragging on for almost two years now, ever since South Carolina had attempted to buy more land from North Carolina. The North had strongly declined, and the South had responded by deploying an army, igniting a war between the two states.

"Okay, war isn't good, but do you know how much we'll get paid?" Thomas said eagerly.

"That's all? That's all you're willing to risk your life in war for?" Ily demanded.

"Well, only because we need the money. With all these dust storms destroying my crops, I can't make a cent anywhere."

"If you have to give up your life for money, then you don't need it that bad," Ily snapped.

"But Ily, don't you see? God has answered our financial worries!"

Ily shot up from her seat. Thomas was a Christian man, but she was shocked by what he was saying.

"I cannot believe you. War is not the answer. God would not send you to war. God would never send anyone to war over financial problems. War *is* a financial problem!"

"Please, don't think of it that way!" Thomas pleaded. "I'm only trying to think of us—our kids, our land, our future!"

Ily looked at Thomas and sighed. She shook her head and walked away to take her frustration out on the dishes.

The next few weeks flew by with a whirlwind of arguments and reconciliations, until seemingly out of nowhere, it came time for Ily to take Thomas to the post office. From there, he would be sent off to the Army.

Upon arrival, they recognized many familiar faces, neighbors and acquaintances from other small towns. Ily saw fathers hugging their young children and kissing their wives goodbye.

Then she noticed her best friend Betsy Ryeson standing with her youngest daughter, Carol, at her feet. Betsy was holding a handkerchief to her eyes while rubbing her baby bump. She was wearing her favorite dress, a brown one dappled with little yellow flowers. Her husband Eddie had gifted it to her during her pregnancy with their youngest of six children—and now, with a seventh on the way, it remained Eddie's favorite as well. Betsy's curly red hair was pinned up with a purple butterfly clip, an heirloom from her grandmother that she always wore when she went out.

Ily glanced around, looking for Eddie as she walked over to grieve with Betsy. Betsy noticed her and met her halfway, wrapping her arms tightly around Ily as she began to bawl even harder.

Meanwhile, Thomas walked over to the check-in table and dropped off his feedbag, which served as his traveling case. He met up with Eddie, and the two talked about the future and what it might bring. Both men were nervous about leaving their wives alone. They had never been apart from their families for this long before, and they were going to miss them terribly.

After checking in, they made their way back to the women. Eddie leaned down to kiss Betsy's belly. Their baby was due in three months.

"Well, this is it," Eddie said. "We're all checked in and everything."

"We'll be departing in a little while. They want to get a head start before the sun sets," Thomas explained.

He turned to Ily.

"Are you going to be alright?" he asked as he embraced her.

Ily looked up at him and nodded. "At least I'll have Betsy and her kids to keep me company."

"And we'll have Ily," Betsy agreed, wiping a tear from her eye.

2

THOMAS

Thomas and Eddie hugged and kissed their wives one final time before climbing into one of the five Army trucks. This location served as one of several designated check-in points for the men. Around thirty soldiers had gathered there, with six assigned to each truck. Thomas and Eddie chose the final truck in the procession so that they could wave to their wives for a little while longer. Once all the men had boarded, the convoy set off for boot camp in Frankfort, Kentucky.

The first day of the journey was already long and exhausting, as most of the terrain was hilly and rocky. The roughest part came when the trucks had to cross a series of rushing rivers. Some of the bridges they encountered hardly looked sturdy enough to support large Army trucks. The river they were approaching now was marked by a sign identifying it as "Las Grandes Aguas Blancas": The Great White Waters.

The truck at the front of the line stopped in front of the bridge, and the driver stepped out to investigate. Walking up to the bridge, he saw a sign that read, "Maximum Weight Capacity 5 Tons". He cautiously stepped onto the first board, losing his balance as it shifted under his foot. Stepping back, he studied the river, noting its width and the speed of the water, which he estimated to be about seven miles per hour.

A second driver caught up to him, and the two muttered to each other, deliberating their next move. Eventually, they nodded in agreement and turned to face the passengers, all of whom were watching the rickety bridge and rushing river with concern.

"Men," the first driver called out, "you'll have to walk across."

"The combined weight of us and the equipment is too much for the bridge to handle," the second driver explained.

The men stood silently as the first driver gingerly eased onto the first board. They winced as the boards popped and slid under the truck's weight, which finally made it across. One by one, the remaining trucks followed, each producing the same unsettling sounds as they crossed the unstable bridge. Then it was the draftees' turn.

Thomas started across with Eddie and the rest of the men. Suddenly, he heard laughter coming from somewhere near the riverbank. He turned toward the sound and saw a young boy in the water, seemingly struggling with something. Thomas kept his eye on the boy and moved closer to the guardrail of the bridge. He watched as the boy reached into the water, almost losing his balance. Alarmed, Thomas leaned forward, accidentally bumping into another draftee. He hastily apologized, but when he looked back, the boy was gone.

Thomas froze, scanning the river anxiously. Then he spotted a head bobbing up and down in the current. Grabbing the guardrail, he acted without hesitation, jumping into the freezing water.

"Oh, my God! What in the—?" Eddie exclaimed as he watched Thomas leap off the bridge. He looked toward the river and spotted the boy.

Eddie shouted to get the drivers' attention and waved them toward Thomas and the boy. One of the drivers grabbed a rope from a truck and ran along the bank to help.

Thomas could hear the boy crying for help as he swam closer. The boy was shouting something, but Thomas couldn't make out the words. His body screamed in protest from the freezing water, but he pushed through the numbness.

Eddie and the driver tried to toss the rope to Thomas and the boy, but their first few attempts failed. Finally, Thomas managed to grab the rope, securing it around himself and the boy. He felt the boy's body trembling as they were pulled to safety.

Once ashore, Thomas and Eddie laid the boy on the ground. Thomas bent down to check his breathing. The boy had fallen unconscious from the cold and exhaustion. Thomas turned him on his side, patting his back in hopes of expelling water from his lungs.

A fellow draftee approached. "Are you two okay?"

Thomas remained silent, focused on the boy.

"I don't think he's going to make it…" Eddie started to say, but he stopped as the boy suddenly began to cough. Water sputtered from his mouth, and everyone sighed in relief.

Thomas leaned down and hugged the boy tightly.

"You had us worried," Eddie chuckled.

"What happened out there?" Thomas asked.

The boy coughed again. "I was skipping rocks, and the next thing I knew, I slipped and got dragged down." He looked at Thomas with sorrowful but grateful eyes.

Thomas wasn't entirely convinced by the boy's story but decided not to press the matter. "What's your name?"

"B-Billy. Billy Jenkins," the boy stammered, still catching his breath.

"Well, Billy, call me Thomas," he said.

"And I'm Eddie," Eddie added with a grin.

"How old are you, anyway?" Thomas asked.

Billy hesitated before replying. "Eighteen."

"That's all well and good," the first driver interjected, "but we're behind schedule now."

"You three can ride in the back of the truck from now on," the second driver added. "We don't need anyone else drowning."

By the time Billy and his rescuers returned to the convoy, everyone had already crossed the bridge. The men climbed back into the trucks, with Eddie, Thomas, and Billy taking a seat in the leading truck.

"So, where you from, kid?" Thomas asked, turning to Billy.

"Douglas, Kansas. My family owns a farm there with my mom, my sister Sarah, and my brother Jason."

"Where's your father?" Eddie asked.

Billy looked away and frowned. Both Thomas and Eddie took the hint.

"Thank you for saving me," Billy said, clearly hoping to change the subject.

Thomas noticed that Billy seemed sad yet eager.

"Billy, are you alright?"

"No. I have to confess something." Billy hesitated. "You know what I said about slipping on a rock and falling?"

Thomas nodded.

"Well, that isn't entirely true. You see, I was trying to catch a fish."

"A *fish*?" Eddie exclaimed. "What in heaven for?"

"Well, you see, my pa taught me how to catch fish, and I was trying to practice. But the current was too strong, and it made me lose my balance."

"Wait, you were practicing? While we were trying to cross?" Thomas asked. "And you were alone?"

"Well, when we—I mean, when I came up to the river, I saw a fish and thought I'd just try until I could cross. And yes, I was alone. Why do you ask?"

"I thought I heard laughter."

Billy looked confused. "What do you mean?"

"Never mind."

"But still—a *fish*?" Eddie repeated, ignoring Thomas's question.

Billy continued. "When I was a little kid, my pa always took me fishin' at our special hole, right down the hill below our house. He taught me everything at that hole—how to swim and hunt and fish.

He could always catch a fish with his bare hands. He tried teaching me, but I could never do it. That is, until the day he died."

He looked down silently.

"I'm so sorry, Billy," Thomas whispered.

"It's okay. It happened two years ago when I was elev—uh, sixteen.

Thomas raised an eyebrow.

"There was a storm coming," Billy continued, "and I had left the barn doors open. My pa went out to shut them. The storm came so fast that when it was over, the barn was gone. Even…even my pa. Everything was gone except our cow, Eliot, who somehow survived. I blamed myself so much that I wouldn't even go to our special fishing hole anymore. 'Til one day, I got the courage and decided to go. I missed my pa, and I wanted some closure. So I went, and I didn't go home until I could catch a fish with my bare hands. And you know what? With the first fish I tried, I caught it. But it didn't feel like I'd done it alone. I felt very close to my pa, and from that moment on, I knew he was with me. I knew I could do whatever I put my mind to, because my pa would be right there with me. And now I know he doesn't blame me, and neither do I," Billy concluded, finally looking up from the ground.

Thomas and Eddie sat in silence, absorbing everything Billy had shared. They felt a deep sense of pity for him but struggled to find the right words.

Meanwhile, Billy remained lost in his own thoughts, reflecting on what he had just revealed. Even he found it hard to believe he had opened up like that. It wasn't often that he spoke about his father or the pain he carried, but now he felt a sense of relief and pride.

"Welcome to Frankfort!" the sign read as the convoy finally reached their destination. Everyone sighed with relief after having made such a short but exhausting trip. They were grateful to meet more of the draftees and acquaint themselves with a few new friends.

They stopped in front of a hotel with another sign that read: "Welcome to Wagon Wheel Hotel! Soldiers Welcome! Rooms Vacant!"

The men piled out and gathered their belongings in front of the hotel as the driver gave instructions.

"Men! This is where you'll be a-stayin' for the night. You can get cleaned up and rested for tomorrow. In the morning you'll get checked into boot camp, which is about a mile from here. There you'll train and get ready for real action. This little road trip has actually given you a small taste of the real training in boot camp—rough terrain, situations where you have to rely on gut instinct."

Thomas noticed the driver eyeing him.

"And walking. Lots and lots of walking," the driver added. He paused and smirked.

"Now! Your rooms are taken care of, but only three to a room. Thank you for your cooperation and for riding peacefully. Please save your anger for the battlefield," the driver concluded, then headed towards the nearest tavern.

"Well, three to a room, that's lucky!" Eddie repeated.

"Yeah, that means I can stay in a room with you guys," Billy said excitedly.

"Nah, I don't think so," Eddie answered. "I think we're gonna find someone else."

Billy's grin instantly fell to shock.

"What? Why—?"

"I'm just joshin' ya," Eddie chuckled. "Of course you're gonna stay with us." They started walking towards the hotel.

"He's not too bright of a boy, is he?" Eddie whispered to Thomas as Billy ran ahead.

"The kid tried to grab a fish with his bare hands in the fastest river in the world. Of course he's not," Thomas agreed.

Thomas and Eddie caught up with Billy and joined him in the line. Thomas looked around, taking in the scene. He watched some of the other men and could tell from their appearances and accents that they were from all different parts of the country.

The hotel looked small, and there was a run-down bar next to it that resembled an old saloon. The bar didn't seem to lack business, as plenty of men were already staggering around outside, trying to get where they were going.

"This is why I don't like big cities," Thomas pointed out as Eddie nodded in agreement. "Ily would never go for a place like this."

"Neither would Betsy."

"Are Ily and Betsy your wives?" Billy asked.

They both nodded.

"Do you have any kids?"

"I don't, but Eddie, on the other hand, has, what—five kids and one on the way?" Thomas asked amusedly.

"*Six* and one on the way!" Eddie corrected with a chuckle. "I have a boy around your age named Noah, another son Charles, a daughter Mary, twin girls Joan and Carrie, then Carol, and a boy or girl soon to be here. So, two boys and four girls so far," he concluded, counting on his fingers. "Noah's seventeen, Charles is fourteen, Mary's ten, Joan and Carrie are eight, Carol is six, and the one on the way is six months along!"

"Wow, that's a lot!" Billy said.

"Well, that's what I get for lovin' children, especially my own. Miss 'em to death right now."

"I can't wait 'til I have some of my own," Thomas said. "I love children, too."

"I'm starting to miss my little brother and sister," Billy sighed. "They'd be getting to their chores right about now."

"Same with my kids," Eddie said. "Charley would be feeding the cows while the twins would be getting in his way, trying to help however they could." He chuckled, remembering his eight-year-old daughters always trying to lend a hand.

They finally reached the doors of the hotel. Walking in, the first thing they noticed was a chandelier with arms shaped like antlers. It hung in the middle of the entryway, glowing enough to light up the front desk, which looked barely big enough for one clerk to squeeze behind.

All of a sudden, they heard: *Bang! Bang!*

"What was that?" Billy yelped.

A man standing ahead of them in line, who had big arms and a bushy mustache, turned to explain. "Gunshots, next door. Get used to it. You're gonna hear 'em all night."

"Really?" Eddie gasped.

The man nodded gruffly.

The line kept moving, and after a few minutes, they reached the front desk.

The man behind the desk was short and had no trouble fitting behind the tight space. He had a ring of hair circling his bald spot, glasses that kept slipping down his nose, and a bushy mustache that almost covered his nostrils. Thomas wondered how the man could even breathe. Then he noticed his name tag, which read: "Welcome to Wagon Wheel Hotel. My name is George."

"Three?" George asked in a soft, low voice.

The three of them leaned forward.

"What?" Eddie asked.

The clerk raised only his eyes from his logbook. "Three?" he repeated, more sternly but still barely audible.

"Yes, three." Thomas said.

"Very well. Room 309. To the right and up the stairs."

George pointed to the room while continuing to write in his books. Thomas and Eddie grabbed the key and their bags, then started toward the stairs. As they walked, Thomas overheard the next group in line.

"What do you mean, you have no more rooms?" exclaimed the tallest man of the group. He had blond, bushy hair and a matching beard.

Thomas stopped and walked back to the desk, hearing George trying to explain himself.

"I'm sorry. I just gave the previous men my last available room," he explained in his quiet voice.

"So, what are we supposed to do? Sleep outside?" the tall man argued.

"No, of course not. Don't be stupid! There's another hotel across the street you can try," George said, standing to his full height, which wasn't much taller than before.

"We've been standing here for an hour waiting for a room, and now you're calling us dumb after telling us to sleep in the street?" The tall man's anger grew as he slammed his fists on the weak plywood desk. The clerk held his things in place as the desk rattled under the impact.

"No, I called you stupid—" George began.

Thomas stepped in beside the man and caught his attention.

"What?" the upset man yelled, turning his body to face Thomas but still glaring at the short clerk.

"Hey, my name's Thomas. I'd be willing to give our room to you three," Thomas offered.

"What? Won't your roommates be mad?"

Thomas glanced back at Eddie and Billy, who both nodded in agreement.

"Well, gee, thanks!" the man said.

Thomas stepped up to the desk clerk and handed the key back to George. As he headed toward the lobby doors, he felt a tap on his shoulder.

"Name's Jo," the blond man said, extending his hand to Thomas.

"Pleasure," Thomas replied, shaking his hand.

Later that evening, after Thomas, Eddie, and Billy had settled in for the night, Thomas sat down to write a letter to Ily. He told her everything about Billy, the journey, and even Jo.

3

ILY

Ily was struggling to stay busy with Thomas gone. Everyone in town and at church had been supporting her, as with all the other families whose men had been drafted. All the older boys in town had stepped up to take their fathers' places and provide for their families.

Not wanting to be home alone, Ily spent most of her time with Betsy and her children, who didn't mind at all; the children loved their 'Aunt' Ily. To make up for all the time she had been spending at Betsy's, Ily had invited them over to her house for supper that Saturday.

"Hello, Ily," Betsy said with a smile as Ily opened the door.

"Hi, Aunt Ily," the children chirped in unison.

"Hello! How are you all?"

"Good. May we go play with Millie?" Carrie asked, already chasing after her siblings, who were running to the barn.

"Yes, you may," Ily called after her, smiling as she wondered what was so fascinating about her old, stubborn cow. Then she turned to Betsy.

"So, Mama, how are you feeling?"

"Like I'm about to burst. This baby should be coming any day now," Betsy said, rubbing her bulging belly. "I think he knows his papa's not around. He keeps trying to feel for his touches, especially at night."

Betsy frowned, realizing how much she missed her loving husband.

"How do you know it's going to be a boy?" Ily asked.

"The same way I knew Noah and Charles were going to be boys," Betsy chuckled. "They all came to me in a dream. When Noah was born, I knew right then and there to trust my dreams. Now, this one didn't come to me directly, but something in my dream told me I'd be having a boy!" Betsy beamed. I've told Eddie about the dreams, and he believes them now too."

The room suddenly fell silent as the women realized how much they missed their husbands.

Ily led the way into the house, and they sat at the kitchen table. They couldn't believe their husbands had only been gone for a week; it felt more like a month.

"It's okay," Ily said, hugging Betsy. "You still have your children to comfort you and keep you busy."

"Yes, but Carol doesn't understand where Daddy is," Betsy said sadly. "She keeps asking where he went and why he's staying away for so long. "I've run out of ways to explain it to her. It constantly reminds me of how much I miss and worry about him." She sat down, grateful to ease her back pain.

"What if I took her for the night?" Ily offered.

Betsy looked up. "What? I can't put you out like that, Ily…"

"Nonsense. It would give you time to spend with your older children, especially before your next little one is due. Plus, Carol will keep me company in this old house. We could bake, draw, and do other fun things. It'd make me feel better, too."

"Are you okay?" Betsy asked.

"I'm not sure. I don't know if I'm just missing Thomas or if it's the dust storms, but my stomach has been acting up. I feel nauseous now and then, and I've been having weird sensations all over. But with all the storms, I think I've just been inhaling too much dirt." Ily laughed a little at her own joke.

"I hope you're alright, Ily. I've been hearing a lot of stories about how the dust is making people sick. You should really get checked out by Dr. Rogers. If you're not feeling well, I don't want Carol putting any stress on you."

"Really, Betsy, I think she'll help keep me distracted from everything happening around us. I want to watch her for the night," Ily insisted, sensing that she was convincing Betsy.

Betsy thought for a moment, then nodded. The two women giggled and hugged. Maybe it would be good for Ily, Betsy thought. They soon called the children in for lunch, and the house was filled with talk and laughter.

Later that evening, Carol's brother Charles brought her to Ily's house with her overnight bag. He explained that their mama was tired from walking earlier, so she'd sent him to deliver Carol. Ily understood and told him to thank his mother again, adding that if she needed anything she'd be happy to help. Charlie nodded and ran the mile and a half back home.

Ily and Carol waved as they watched him disappear over the hill before heading back inside.

"Well, Carol, what would you like to do first?" Ily asked, crouching down to Carol's height.

"Where's my daddy?" asked the precious hazel-eyed little girl.

"Your daddy is with my husband. They had to go away for a while with other daddies and husbands. But don't worry, they'll look after each other and be back soon, hopefully." Ily watched the little girl as she spoke, trying to see if she understood.

"Mama always gets sad when I ask her. Do you get sad, too?" Carol whispered.

"Yes, I'm always thinking about Uncle Thomas, and I miss him very much," Ily said. "That's why I like to bake or sew—anything to keep busy." She tried to smile and noticed Carol deep in thought.

"How about apple pie?" Carol smiled, moving on to the next thing on her six-year-old mind.

It took the rest of the afternoon to roll out the dough, peel and cut the apples, and wash the used dishes. After putting the pie on the windowsill to cool, they started on supper. When they were finished eating their chicken dumplings, mashed potatoes, and a piece of their delicious pie, the girls fell into bed, thanking the Lord for a great day and praying for their loved ones.

The next morning, Ily and Carol rose early to start on chores. They collected eggs from the squawking hens to make sunny-side-up eggs with porridge. Then Ily allowed Carol to help with other easy chores around the house. They finished with some sweet tea while sitting on the front porch, relaxing before they headed to take Carol back home.

Ily took a deep breath of the warm fresh air as she sat watching Carol pick dandelions that somehow grew out of the dirt. Ily shielded her eyes from the sun as Carol came running up, handing her the weeds.

"Beautiful, Carol."

Carol flashed a smile before running off to scrounge for more, almost bumping into Mr. Kay. He gave the usual greeting and then was off again to deliver more mail. Ily rummaged through her own mail for a letter from Thomas. Not finding anything, she went inside to start packing Carol's belongings, along with the pie.

It was a lovely day, and Betsy's house was just over two hills, so Ily and Carol decided to travel there on foot, walking hand-in-hand.

On their way, they passed the old shed that stood alone on the top of the hill. Ily had always been fascinated by the shed, which had only a tiny window on one side and a door barely hanging onto its hinges. It had been abandoned for a long time, and no one knew who had built it or how it was still standing after so many years.

They reached the top of the second hill when the air suddenly turned noticeably cooler. Looking down at Betsy's farm, Ily noticed something dark in the distance. It was a sight that was all too familiar: a dark cloud of dirt stretching across the horizon for miles. Ily had seen so many storms before, but her gut told her that this one would be more aggressive than any other.

She suddenly noticed how fast the air had turned from warm and humid to an almost cool breeze, which began blowing sand and dirt into their eyes. The sky and earth looked like they were being swallowed up into complete black emptiness.

Birds squawked as they flew away. All went silent almost immediately as the storm headed straight toward them. Ily scooped Carol up and started running down the hill toward Betsy's house, hoping to reach safety. But halfway down the hill, she stopped and watched in horror as the storm blew in and blocked her view of the house.

Ily frantically turned back, still carrying Carol, not even realizing that she was also lugging along her knapsack and the pie. As they reached the top of the hill, she looked back just in time to see the dust starting to cover the hill, creeping faster and faster toward them. The wind continued throwing sand and dirt into Ily's eyes, but she knew they were almost to the shed. The storm engulfed the rest of the sky, plunging them into darkness.

Ily hit the shed hard, almost dropping Carol, but quickly recovered and scrambled against the wooden structure. Dirt stung her eyes and she squeezed them shut. She choked as the dust smothered her nose and mouth. She tried even harder to cover Carol's nose and mouth with the skirt of her dress.

In the dark, Ily felt the cold, rough surface of the shed with her free hand, pushing against the walls as she searched for the door. She struggled around the shed two times—or maybe it was three; she couldn't tell in the pitch blackness—before finally feeling the indent of the door frame. She fumbled for the knob and finally stumbled across the threshold.

With the storm still blowing hard at her back, Ily immediately sat Carol down, along with everything else she'd been carrying, then pressed her back against the door. She pushed backward with all her might, begging for the door to obey her until it miraculously slammed shut against the raging storm.

She leaned against the door, panting. As she wiped her eyes, it took her a moment to realize that her vision was not the problem—the storm had plunged the world into complete darkness. She couldn't see anything in front of her, not even her own hand when she touched her nose.

Dirt still pelted her face. Suddenly, she remembered the tiny window and figured a pane must be broken, allowing dirt to come in uninvited. She fell to the ground, searching for the knapsack to stuff into the window, hoping to block out the dirt and drown out the roar of the wind. Carol started crying and coughing as Ily crawled toward her.

Ily took the skirt of her dress and carefully wiped Carol's face clean, murmuring words of comfort. She then wiped her own face. Her nose and eyes stung from the dirt. They were both too weak, their throats too sore, to say much of anything. All they could do was hold each other, listening to the howl of the wind and the tiny grains of dirt hitting the shed's exterior.

To distract Carol, Ily offered her a piece of pie, hoping it might bring her some comfort. They could tell by the taste that the pie had a coating of dirt on it, but not enough to waste the treat. After finishing it, they fell fast asleep on a pile of dirt, utterly exhausted.

Ily was awakened by a beam of light shining through a hole in the wall. The howling wind had fallen silent. The storm had passed.

She stood up, a sheet of dirt sliding off her dress. She peered down at Carol, seeing that she, too, was covered in a blanket of debris.

Ily struggled to keep her balance, slipping slightly on the layers of grime that covered the floor. She made her way to the window to try to look outside, but the dirt had piled up over it, allowing only the slightest bit of sunlight to shine through the cracks.

"At least we weren't buried alive under the walls of this shed," she muttered to herself.

A small avalanche of dirt rushed in as she pulled the knapsack from the window to peek outside. The sun was bright, and the sky was clear—no sign of the chaos from the day before. The scene outside appeared eerily innocent, as though nothing extraordinary had occurred just a few hours prior.

Ily wondered how long the storm had lasted, but her thoughts were interrupted when Carol began coughing. She turned to the child and gently helped her to her feet.

"You ready to go home?" Ily asked.

Carol nodded.

More dirt poured in as they pulled the door open, covering their feet.

Off in the distance, Ily could barely make out her own house and barn, which had also been buried almost to their roofs. She began to mourn the amount of work it would take to clean up, but she couldn't focus on that now. She had to get Carol back to her family and make sure they were all alive and safe.

Starting on their way back to Betsy's house, Ily gazed sadly at Thomas's crops, which had been leveled—again. Thomas would be upset about seeing that, she thought to herself, lamenting the scene herself.

At the top of the second hill, Ily could see Betsy sweeping by the front door, with the younger ones running around, acting like they were helping. As Ily and Carol neared the house, Betsy noticed them and began running towards them, shouting her praises at the top of her lungs. Carol ran to meet her mother halfway, and Betsy scooped her up as best as she could manage with her bulging belly.

"Are you two alright?" Betsy exclaimed.

"I think we are. I'm so glad to see you guys are okay," Ily started, shaking with weariness and relief. "We got stranded in that old shed all night when that awful dust storm came. We just barely made it to that shed before the storm swept over us."

"Oh, my goodness, I'm so sorry!" Betsy hugged Ily. "Charles saw it while he was playing outside. He ran in and alerted us to take cover."

Carol interrupted with a coughing fit.

"You might want to get her checked out," Ily said. "I feel so awful. I didn't know it was coming. I thought we could run to your house in time, but your place just disappeared, so we turned back around running," she apologized, sobbing.

"It's okay. I understand. I'm just glad you're both safe," Betsy comforted her.

"I hope we are. I think I'm going to get checked out by Dr. Rogers, too. I haven't been sleeping well, and my stomach has been hurting a lot lately."

"Well, come in for a while and rest! I'll get you two some water and something to eat," Betsy said, putting her arm around Ily to assist her to the house. Each of the children ran up to them to give them hugs, shedding tears of joy.

Everyone liked Dr. Almanzo Rogers. He did his work out of the kindness of his heart, taking whatever payment his patients could afford, which was usually homemade food. He was always sympathetic, especially during a time like this. With the Depression ongoing, about half the town had become vacant, as no one could afford to stay without a job.

Ily walked into the small wooden office, which Dr. Rogers had built himself next to his house just inside of town. The office was just big enough for a wall desk, a couple of waiting chairs, and a curtain leading to a small examining room in the back.

Ily stood waiting by the desk next to the chairs, which were already full. A woman cradling a baby boy sat in one while a little girl sat beside her. The little girl, who looked to be about eight years old, wore a blue dress that was covered in dust and dirt. Her blonde hair was now mostly brown, and Ily realized sadly that she must have also been caught in yesterday's storm, which was now causing her to cough and sneeze.

The mother was holding her baby close to her chest, her eyes red from crying, muttering under her breath. She kept her gaze fixed on the floor and didn't acknowledge Ily's presence when she stepped inside. Ily didn't recognize the woman; even in a small town like theirs, people had been moving in and out, hoping for a better life.

Ily turned her attention to a newspaper sitting on the desk. She glanced at the date: Monday, April 15, 1935, the day after the big storm. Scanning the headlines, she read the bold text: *Black Sunday Turns Day into Night.*

She read on anxiously, seeing headlines like *Dust Victims Pray for Oklahoma Rain,* and *Farmers Blamed for Cause of Dust Storms; Richness of Soil Blown Away.* She scoffed, offended on Thomas's behalf.

The next article startled her: *Huge Dust Cloud, Blown 1,500 Miles, Dims City for Five Hours.* Before she could process the shocking news, she jumped at the sound of the curtain being pulled back as Dr. Rogers stepped out of the examining room. He noticed her immediately.

"Oh, hello, Ily. How are you today?" he greeted her with a faint but delighted smile.

Ily noticed that his dark hair was disheveled, not in its usual neat, short ponytail. The exhaustion was evident in his eyes.

Ily returned his smile and was about to greet him when a loud, brash voice interrupted her. A woman barged out from behind the curtain, oblivious to anyone else's presence. Ily immediately recognized the flowing blonde hair and haughty demeanor: it was none other than Alice, Dr. Rogers' ex-wife.

Alice's family, the Wilburs, were the wealthiest in town, and Alice made sure everyone knew it. She was never shy about seeking attention. She had divorced Dr. Rogers and blamed him for it, despite having had an affair with the town's blacksmith, Russel Owens. Now, she was carrying Russel's baby and, ironically, had chosen Dr. Rogers to be her obstetrician.

"So, the next appointment is in two weeks?" Alice asked, rubbing her stomach. Ily noticed she wasn't even showing yet.

"Yes, two weeks, Alice," Dr. Rogers replied, his tone tinged with annoyance.

"Well!" Alice exclaimed, flabbergasted. "Almanzo, you don't have to get all snippy about it. This child could have been yours." She headed for the door.

"Goodbye, Alice. I have other patients waiting," he said, giving Ily a wink.

Alice turned back just in time to catch the wink. She scoffed and stomped out the door.

"So, how can I help you, Ily? How's Thomas?" Dr. Rogers asked, holding the curtain aside for her.

"Um, is everything okay?" Ily asked, hesitating to move.

"Yes, fine—except for the dust storms. Sad, scary things," he answered. "Oh, with Alice? Well, that could always be better."

Ily glanced at the mother and daughter still sitting in the waiting room. "Shouldn't you see them first? They were here before me. She looks very sick," she said, referring to the little girl, who wore a sad expression on her face.

"I've already seen them. They're just waiting, deciding what to do next. If you're ready, we can get started before more patients arrive. I have a feeling I'll be busy for a good while, thanks to that terrible storm," he said, continuing to hold the curtain open for her.

As Ily stepped by the mother still clutching her baby, she finally caught what the woman had been muttering: "I blame you." The words were directed at her weary daughter.

It was then that Ily noticed the baby boy lying motionless in the woman's arms.

"So, how are you feeling today?" Dr. Rogers asked as he closed the curtain behind them.

"Not too good, I suppose. Lately, my stomach has been hurting, I've been feeling nauseated, and I toss and turn at night. And yesterday, Carol—Betsy's youngest—and I got caught in that horrible storm."

Dr. Rogers had been putting on his gloves, but he suddenly whirled around to face her.

"What? Were you two able to take cover?" He motioned urgently for Ily to sit on the examination table at the back of the room.

"Yes, we hid in a shed—hopefully in time," Ily replied, sitting on the table. "But with all the dirt swirling around us, I couldn't believe I'd managed to open and shut the door against the wind. We were on our way back to Betsy's house when we got caught. I made sure we had our heads covered and everything, but I'm just so afraid it wasn't enough. Carol started coughing a lot, and Betsy agreed that we should bring her in to see you to make sure she's fine."

Dr. Rogers looked worried. "Have they been in yet?"

"No, I haven't seen them. But if I don't, I might just go check on them before the day is out."

"Well, I hope to see them soon. Thank you for letting me know about little Carol."

Ily nodded. "Of course."

"Well, alright, let's check you out," Dr. Rogers said, gesturing for Ily to lie down. He began pressing gently on her stomach.

Ily glanced around the small room. Only two people could fit comfortably standing by the table. One window offered a view of the nearby school, while the adjacent wall housed a cabinet and a sink beside a counter cluttered with test tubes and needles.

"When your stomach hurts, do you feel anything specific? Can you describe the pain?" Dr. Rogers asked, retrieving his stethoscope.

"Maybe…It feels like cramps but not, if that makes sense."

Dr. Rogers nodded as he put the earbuds in and listened to Ily's heart and stomach, remaining a good while on the latter.

"Ah-huh!" he finally exclaimed, smiling. "Well, Ily, you seem to be in very good condition," he announced.

"Oh, I'm so glad!" Ily replied with relief as she sat up.

"Nothing that can't be cured in about eight months."

"Eight months?"

"Yes, very good condition," Dr. Rogers repeated, his smile growing even wider. "Very, very good condition. As is your baby."

"My—wait, what?"

"I am happy to announce that you're pregnant, Ily."

"But how? I mean, when?" Tears blurred Ily's vision.

"It seems Thomas didn't want you to be lonely while he was away," Dr. Rogers chuckled.

"Oh, my goodness, I can't believe it's finally happened! We've been trying ever since we got married seven years ago, and now I'm finally pregnant!"

Dr. Rogers walked Ily back to the waiting room. She barely noticed that the mother and daughter had left the office, but she did see Betsy and her five children approaching through the window.

Ily could hardly wait to share the blessed news. She opened the door for them but stopped herself, her concern for Carol taking precedence. She let Dr. Rogers take Betsy and Carol into the examining room while the rest of the children played outside. Ily sat in the waiting room, anxious to hear about Carol. As she waited, she read another article: *Cold Wave Hits Midwestern States!*

"A cold front clashed with warm air over the Midwest, dropping temperatures by more than thirty degrees," the article explained. "The wind whipped into a frenzy, creating a wall of dust and dirt hundreds of miles wide and thousands of feet high. The storm has claimed around 7,000 lives due to illnesses like dust pneumonia, and about 250,000 people have decided to flee the plains. The Black Blizzard has painted the central plains in shades of black and white, leaving the earth barren."

Ily was still processing the grim facts when Betsy and Carol returned.

"How is she, Betsy?" Ily asked, jumping to her feet.

Betsy shook her head slowly. "She has it," she said softly. "She has dust pneumonia."

Ily gasped. "I—I'm so sorry. It's all…"

Betsy stopped her. "It's not your fault. You didn't know; how could you have? You were too far from your house and couldn't reach mine. You did what you could."

Lowering her head, Betsy walked out the door. Ily watched through the window as Betsy told her children the news, their smiles slowly fading.

Standing on the porch, Ily felt a wave of guilt wash over her, knowing that deep down, Betsy blamed her.

4

THOMAS

Boot camp was exactly as Thomas had imagined: a chaotic sprawl of tents, bustling men, and constant shouting. Lines stretched outside various buildings and tables scattered around the camp. Some men in line struggled to juggle the gear and clothing they had just been issued, while others, already dressed in their uniforms, stood in formation practicing stances with their arms clasped behind their backs and their feet planted wide apart.

Thomas noticed rows of tents marked with a large sign reading "Bunkers." To their right stood a few larger, more polished tents bearing signs that read "Mess Hall" and "Office." Behind it all was a field with a track surrounding an obstacle course.

Thomas and his friends were surrounded by the sound of shouting echoing throughout the camp, commands for marching and various stances being barked out. Thomas led the way over to a table where a tall man with blond, buzzed hair and a stern look was standing. He'd barely reached the table before the man boomed, "Last name?"

"Milton."

The man shuffled through his papers. "Milton, you're checked in. Bunk 13, color red. Next!" The stern man stared past Thomas at Eddie.

"Ryeson, sir." Eddie saluted, struggling to hide his smirk. The man looked at Eddie in disgust, then rummaged through his papers again.

"Ryeson, you're checked in. Bunk 13, color red," the man repeated, already motioning for Billy to step forward. Eddie maintained his salute as he shuffled over to Thomas. The man at the table rolled his eyes.

"Jenkins," Billy said confidently, stepping up to the table.

"You're checked in. Bunk 13, color red."

As they made their way to the next line, Eddie started laughing. "Hey, did you see the way he looked at me?"

"Eddie, this isn't really the place to joke around. Everyone would want us to take war seriously," Thomas insisted.

Eddie turned around and began walking backwards. "I know, and I will. I just want to have a little more fun before the more serious stuff happens."

The barber line shortened as they made their way there; only a few men were standing outside the tent flaps, while others made their way out, beardless and nearly bare-headed.

"Looks like they chopped it all off," Eddie pointed out nervously, rubbing his beard and running his hand through his own hair.

"Yeah, well, I guess it's required," Thomas said. "Ily would agree with a little trim."

They approached the front of the line and were able to get in together, sitting in three of the four chairs that were lined up. The barbers then began their transformations.

"You ready? Won't take long," the barber mumbled to Thomas.

Thomas barely nodded before the barber stopped him and began snipping his hair away.

A few minutes later, their haircuts completed, Thomas and Eddie stepped outside.

"Woah, Eddie, is that you?" Thomas said.

"Yeah, well, you should take a look at yourself, Thomas," Eddie teased. Their matching long, bushy manes had both been reduced to a buzz. Their laughter was tinged with sadness as they both realized that they would no longer be able to tie their hair behind their heads.

"Where's Billy?" Eddie asked. "I wonder what he looks like." They both looked around. "Where *is* that boy?" Eddie put his hands on his hips.

They finally noticed a man standing a few feet away who also seemed to be looking for someone.

"Wait a minute—*Billy*? Is that you?" Thomas exclaimed, dumb-founded by Billy's new look.

"Man, you don't look like a boy no more," Eddie said in awe.

"Well, isn't that what the army is supposed to do? Turn boys into men?" Billy asked with a grin, feeling relieved as he thought to himself: *I might actually be able to pull this off.*

"I guess so!" his friends agreed.

Next, they found the tent where they were to collect their uniforms, helmets, and survival gear. They were each handed an olive-green jacket with matching pants, along with a pair of khakis and a white under-shirt. Their gear included a combat helmet, knee and elbow pads, a canteen, a sleeping bag, a bulletproof vest, a rifle, and a knapsack to carry it all in. After gathering their equipment, they headed to the bun-kers to find their temporary home for the next few weeks.

As they reached the three rows of bunkhouses, they followed the number plates above the tent flaps, maneuvering past other men also searching for their bunks. They found number 13 near the end of the third row.

"I wonder how many men to a bunker?" Billy wondered as they walked in.

"Thirteen bunk beds on both walls," Eddie counted. "So, twenty-six all together."

"Thirteen bunkhouses with twenty-six beds—that's three hundred and thirty-eight men altogether, give or take," Thomas calculated.

They noticed two unclaimed bunks next to each other by the window. Thomas knew he would enjoy bunking by a window, especially since it faced the direction of home. He thought about Ily and wondered what she was doing right now—probably feeding Millie or sitting in her chair, reading one of her favorite books, while twirling a lock of her golden-brown hair.

"What're you smiling at, old boy?" Eddie asked, throwing his gear up onto the top bunk.

"Oh, nothing. Just thinking of Ily," Thomas replied, moving forward to join them. "Can't help but think about her being alone in that old house, especially when the dust storms hit."

"I'm sure Betsy and the kids are keeping her busy, and if she needs any help, Betsy will let her stay with her."

After settling in and changing into their uniforms, they headed back outside to the formation lines to await the next instruction.

Thomas, Eddie, and Billy joined a growing group of men forming rows under an American flag, with a sign displaying their bunk number and color. All their attention turned to watch a tall, muscular man pacing back and forth in front of them. He wore a brown hat with a wide brim that hid his bare head from the sun, and he was dressed in a beige uniform.

"All y'all listen up now, ya hear?" the sergeant yelled in a deep Kentucky accent. "You men are in the army now. My army. Y'all ain't at home anymore, where your mommies or wives can babysit you and tend to your every need. There will be no babysitting here. Understood?"

A few men nodded in acknowledgment, ready for action, while others stood glued to their spots, frozen in fear. The sergeant glared down at the men's faces one by one. Thomas noticed that the sergeant's face had turned red, but he couldn't tell whether it was from the strain of yelling or the light of the blazing sun.

"Alright, now. My name is Sergeant Dow, and you will answer to me over the next nine weeks."

Sergeant Dow paused and looked around.

"There's about twenty-six men here in this group. Over the next couple of weeks, half of you will come with me, and the other half will go with this sergeant."

All eyes followed Dow's hand as he extended it toward a slightly larger and younger man, who stepped forward next to him. For how big he was, Thomas was surprised he hadn't noticed him before.

"This here is Sergeant Swoop," Dow said.

In his peripheral vision, Thomas saw Eddie bite back a smile.

Sergeant Swoop seemed too young to be leading a group of men, yet he appeared stronger than most of the other sergeants training the newly drafted recruits. His muscles seemed to almost burst out of his white shirt.

"Swoop will be helping me keep an eye on everyone's training," Sergeant Dow continued. "He may look young, but don't let that deceive you—he can take a person down in less than a minute, so I reckon you better get along with your bunkmates."

Dow continued pacing back and forth, his hands clasped behind his back. "Now that introductions are over, it's time to get down to the real business. This is what's fixin' to happen over the next nine weeks. There are three phases to get through: Red, White, and Blue. Each phase lasts three weeks, and at the end of each one there will be a ceremony during which you'll demonstrate what you've learned. Phase Red will train you to navigate the land, read maps, and use compasses. That way, in case you get lost, you'll know how to make your way back to camp. And remember, no wandering off! Sergeant Swoop, tell them why."

"Don't go wandering off because you might end up in enemy territory and get captured or killed," Sergeant Swoop replied. He, too, spoke with a Southern drawl, though it wasn't as deep as Sergeant Dow's.

"Thank you, Swoop. Did y'all understand all that? Now, Phase Two, White: you will learn to shoot, to defend and protect yourself.

You'll also focus on aiming and shooting with different types of weapons you might encounter. You'll practice loading, unloading, throwing grenades, cleaning weapons, and even more marching and physical training. And finally, the last phase, Blue. You're going to need to pass our physical fitness test on the obstacle course, qualify your rifle, and handle grenades. Then we'll reckon if you're qualified to run with the big dogs, and protect your fellow soldiers. You'll need to pass every test required to survive in the real game of war."

Sergeant paused and looked around the room. "Now, last but not least: during all of your training, chores will be assigned each week. The same chore for everyone will be to keep your sleeping quarters clean, be well-shaven, and practice good hygiene. There won't always be time to shower when you feel like it, so keep your uniform clean. I reckon I've made myself clear?"

"Sir, yes, sir!" the crowd shouted in unison.

Dow looked over at Swoop.

"Do you have anything else to add, Sergeant?"

"Always follow orders and no goofing off."

"Good reminder, Swoop. Anyone who throws a hissy fit or thinks he's a clown will learn very quickly why we do not tolerate any of those behaviors. If there are no questions, I say we start off with our morning marches."

Sergeant Dow began to turn away from the crowd.

Eddie raised his hand.

"Yes, sir?" Dow said.

"What about mail?" Eddie asked.

"Mail arrives every Tuesday or Wednesday. Any more questions?" He paused. "No? Good!"

Over the next several weeks, Sergeant Dow pushed the men to their limits, and every night, Thomas fell onto his lumpy mattress, savoring every minute of sleep. He'd thought he was strong and fit, but after running and marching for six miles and jumping through hoops and over hurdles, he realized he wasn't nearly fit enough. He had never felt so sore and achy, even after a full day in the fields. Some nights, he fell asleep dreaming of home and yearning for his wife.

Each morning, a whistle blew to wake the men up. Once, Eddie tried sleeping in but was thrown out of the bunk by Sergeant Swoop. Thomas always jumped out of bed, too startled to even think about returning to sleep, but he would regret it soon after, wishing to rest his sore muscles.

They were slowly getting used to their new routine. Each day began with making beds, brushing teeth, shaving, and dressing for roll call. They marched to roll call, even though they weren't in formation. They had to march everywhere they went: to their bunk tents, the mess hall, training courses, and even the lavatory.

After roll call, they marched to the half-mile track for a warm-up run of five laps followed by stretches, before marching to the mess hall for breakfast. Following each meal would be more training and marching until the end of the day.

They were trained to utilize the land for camouflage, enabling them to conceal themselves in case of injury. They also learned to rely on the land for sourcing food and constructing shelters. When they weren't training or marching, they spent time in a classroom memorizing maps of the camp and the surrounding backwoods, preparing to defend every area when they reached the battlefield. For all the time they spent familiarizing themselves with the terrain, they had yet to see the camp and battlefield in person.

Every night ended at twenty-one hundred, just before lights-out an hour later, when the men would be turned loose to enjoy a little free time before collapsing into their bunks. Thomas, Eddie, and Billy eagerly anticipated their personal time. It was their chance to unwind after a grueling day of training, when they could finally catch up on reading and writing letters. Thomas didn't miss any opportunity to write to Ily.

The days of training started to blur together. Sergeant Dow emphasized the importance of adhering to a strict schedule and maintaining constant order. He also cautioned that this week—filled with laps, hurdles, and marches—would be the easiest of their entire nine-week training period. The men quickly learned to stifle their complaints.

One night, as they were eating dinner, Thomas and his friends, along with a couple of other draftees, were sitting at a table near Sergeants Dow and Swoop when two men walked up to them.

"Sergeant Dow, sir?" one of the men addressed with a salute.

"Stand down, Private Kelly. There's no need to salute at the table," Sergeant Dow answered in his deep Southern accent. "What can I do for you?"

Private Kelly lowered his hand as the other man, Private Jack, stood beside him with his arms tucked behind his back. They were the same height, both around five foot eight, but Jack's narrow, rounded shoulders made him appear smaller than his counterpart.

"Private Jack and I just wanted to know when we're going to get to the real training," Kelly said. "You know, the obstacle course and the weapon training?"

"Damn, boy, it's only been a couple of weeks, and you've already forgotten what I said about the training schedule," Sergeant Dow chuckled. "Why are you in such a rush, anyhow? It's just gonna get a lot tougher from here on out."

"Nothing's too hard for me, Sergeants."

Swoop smiled sarcastically and rolled his eyes before looking back down at his food.

"All in due time, but for now, just relax while you still can—'cause believe me, son, when you're out there for real, you're going to wish you hadn't been in such a rush."

"Can you believe Kelly and Jack? Ever since we got here, they've been doing everything like they've done it before," Eddie said to

Thomas as they marched with Billy to the track to begin their assigned exercises for the afternoon.

Thomas answered with a shake of his head.

"Talk about a teacher's pet," Billy chimed in.

Both Thomas and Eddie gave Billy a confused look.

"A what?" they asked in unison.

"You know, a teacher's pet. Someone who tries to be better than everyone else so the teacher likes 'em more," Billy explained. "Although, I don't think the sergeants think very kindly of Kelly and Jack. They're always trying to do things before Sergeant Dow even tells anyone to do them. I know a couple in my grade—bullies, they are."

Billy swallowed hard, realizing what he had just said and hoping that Eddie and Thomas hadn't caught on. He finally let out a sigh of relief as they both nodded in agreement.

"It gets the bullies into more trouble than if they would just listen in the first place," Thomas said.

"Yeah, that would be Jack and Kelly," said Eddie. "Except I wouldn't call 'em teacher's pets—more like army brats."

"I wonder why he goes by Kelly, anyway, and not his first name," Billy mused.

"Who knows?" Eddie shrugged indifferently.

The weeks flew by as the first phase of training came to an end, and most draftees agreed that it had been relatively easy. It was hard to believe that the ceremony for the completion of Phase Red had already arrived; even the sergeants were surprised at how quickly the weeks had gone by. The ceremony was set for Wednesday, April tenth, and the men were eager to demonstrate to the sergeants what they had learned.

The draftees were woken up at 0500 to prepare for the day. Thomas noticed that Kelly was already standing at the end of his bed with his buddy Jack, waiting for Sergeant Dow to inspect their bunks.

Sergeant Swoop was the first inside the bunkhouse, and he shifted to allow Sergeant Dow to step in beside him.

"Alright, men," Dow began. "Today, as y'all may know, is Ceremony Day. Today is where you will show us what you've learned in the last three weeks. Congratulations on making it this far."

Once the ceremony began, the draftees demonstrated to the sergeants how well they had mastered the survival techniques they'd learned, proving that they were prepared for any situation they might face. Both sergeants were pleased to see that most of the group passed the first phase.

Phase Two began with the usual morning routine, which the draftees had quickly grown accustomed to. This phase focused on advanced weapon handling and more intense physical training. Thomas, Eddie, Billy, Jack, Kelly, and two dozen other men continued training under Sergeant Swoop. To kick things off, Swoop led them to the obstacle course. As they approached, Thomas noticed that the course resembled a massive playground, complete with monkey bars, slides, hanging ropes, tires, and other unfamiliar obstacles.

"We want to see how physically capable y'all are and identify where you need to improve," Sergeant Swoop explained. "On the battlefield, you can't afford to be slowed down by your own weaknesses. Here's how it works: start at the low wall, then move to the rope swings and cross over the mud pit. After that, climb over the five-foot wall, crawl through the tunnel, jump over hurdles, and cross the monkey bars. Then it's over and under the wires, stepping through every other tire, scaling the nine-foot wall with the rope, and finishing with another set of rope swings. Got it? Now go!"

Thomas joined the others, sprinting toward the course. He lined up at the low wall, watching as most of the men hoisted themselves over with ease. When his turn came, Thomas strained to scale the wall, but he, along with a few others, couldn't make it over and was forced to run around it to continue.

Thomas then reached the two tunnels, and he felt himself being shoved into the first. Each man surged ahead, crawling inside before the draftee ahead of him could fully enter. Thomas made it through quickly.

The hurdles and monkey bars posed no challenge for him, as he'd grown familiar with them during the previous week's training. At the tires, he noticed several men running too quickly, tripping and falling face-first, causing a chain reaction of tumbles. One man ahead of Billy hit the ground hard and began bleeding from his nose, but it didn't slow him down—he simply pulled himself off the ground and kept running.

Eddie caught up to Thomas, and they waited in line to climb the rope and scale the next wall. While some struggled and were forced to go around yet again, Thomas and Eddie managed to hoist themselves up with the rope's help. They pressed on to the final obstacle: the rope swing over the mud pit.

Thomas watched as the men ahead of him either made it across unscathed or fell, emerging completely covered in mud. Eddie was already ahead, swinging confidently from rope to rope. But just as he reached for the final rope, he lost his grip and fell straight into the mud pit.

Then it was Thomas's turn. He rubbed the sweat from his hands onto his pants, grabbed the rope, and launched off the platform. One swing at a time, he moved carefully, grasping each rough rope until his feet landed safely on the opposite platform. He had made it through the entire obstacle course clean, aside from some dust from having crawled under the wires.

Thomas walked over to Eddie, who was furiously wiping mud off his slowly drying uniform.

"You alright?" Thomas asked.

"Yeah, yeah, yeah. Let's all laugh at the mud monster," Eddie grumbled.

"Woah, what's the matter with you?"

"You! Of all people, you didn't fall in! Even Kelly fell in."

"Well, that's because he tried showing off by doing it one hand at a time," Thomas replied with a shrug.

"Whatever," Eddie muttered as he walked off.

"Jeez, what's wrong with him?" Billy asked as he joined Thomas, wringing mud from his clothes. "Oh, wow, Thomas, you didn't fall in the mud? Nice."

The following day, Sergeant Swoop took Thomas and the rest of the group to the classroom to begin his lecture about marksmanship and weaponry.

"Now, men, you are going to learn in a short session the regulations, guidelines, and safety rules of weaponry. You'll learn how dangerous rifles and hand grenades really can be. The number one rule, of course, is no goofing off; this is not a game! Marksmanship is very serious and could very well mean your life or someone else's. Never point weapons at one another. If you do, you will highly regret it, for there are no second chances. Plus, you are here to look after your fellow soldiers. We don't need any friendly fire now, ya hear?"

Swoop lectured for a few hours about the history of firearms, the range of models, and the types of ammunition. He modeled a handgun, a short rifle, and a hand grenade. He talked about safety, accuracy, and the fundamentals of shooting, and showed the men how to disassemble, reassemble, load, and use each weapon. Thomas's group was taught proper stances and shooting positions, ensuring they could handle each firearm comfortably. They also learned about sight alignment, trigger control, and managing their breathing—an essential skill for maintaining composure while aiming.

"After neutralizing an enemy," Swoop continued, "take a moment before advancing to ensure the area is secure and there is no more life to be had from that enemy. Continuously evaluate the situation. Keep your focus on the end of your weapon until the shot is fired. Do not take your eyes off the target, or you very well could be the one who perishes."

Thomas and Eddie shared a glance, a hint of fear in their eyes.

Swoop led them to the mess hall for the afternoon meal following the morning training.

"Now, team, remember all that and you should make it out alive, for a while, anyway. Now go eat, and afterwards we will continue with more drills."

Over the next two weeks, the men pushed themselves to their limits. Whenever they weren't on the shooting range refining their marksmanship, or in the classroom studying weapons and self-defense, they practiced on the obstacle course, determined to conquer it.

Soon, it was already Ceremony Day, and the men were excited once again to show the sergeants what they had worked hard for: to prove that they could run through the course without falling, to demonstrate their weapon skills and tactics, and to display their marching and salutes.

Most of the men ran the obstacle course perfectly, even Eddie, with only a handful of the men dirtying their uniforms. Some men still couldn't climb over the walls, but many of them flew across the mud pits. Kelly even made it, still eager to show off.

At supper, the sergeants told their groups how each of them had performed. Sergeant Dow stood in front.

"Y'all came here to learn how to become men, and most of y'all succeeded in doing just that. I am pleased to tell y'all that you've passed Phase Two. Congratulations. Tomorrow we will begin Phase Three, during which you'll be focusing on everything you've learned during the last six weeks of training."

A week had passed since the beginning of Phase Three. The men were becoming familiar with the functions of each weapon and the proper stances to adopt when handling their rifles.

Eddie was staring into space when Thomas entered the bunkhouse. He walked over to Eddie and sat next to him.

"You alright?" Thomas asked.

"I don't know. I just miss my family, I guess," Eddie said softly, continuing to stare into space.

"Hey, guys," Billy shouted as he entered the bunk. "The whole Midwest just got hit by a bad dust storm—like, *really* bad. Everything got buried deep."

"What? Where'd you learn that?" Thomas asked, stunned.

"Mail came. It's in the paper, too."

Thomas and Eddie hurried to grab their mail, tearing open their letters as they made their way back to their bunks. They were so anxious that they couldn't even sit down to read them.

"Oh, good, Ily's okay," Thomas sighed as he read the letter. "She went to the doctor for a checkup and found out…" His eyes widened as he continued reading. "Oh, my."

"What is it, Tom?" Eddie asked, glancing up from his own four-page letter.

Thomas looked up, meeting Eddie's gaze with a twinkle in his eye.

"I'm going to be a father," he said tearily.

"Well, congratulations, boy! 'Bout time, too!" Eddie laughed and hugged Thomas.

They sat down and continued reading their own letters. From the corner of his eye, Thomas noticed Eddie's expression growing somber.

"Everything alright?"

"Can't say it is. Carol has dust…pe-nemona."

"Pe-nemona? Oh, pneumonia?" Thomas corrected.

"Yeah, Betsy says she's not doing well, and she's only getting worse. She has a high fever, coughing up mucus and mud, and sleeping all the time. The doctor has been putting ice on her to bring her temperature down. Oh, Thomas, how could this have happened?" Eddie's voice cracked.

"Ily says she feels terrible," Thomas replied, reading his own letter.

"Ily? What's Ily got to do with Carol getting dust…dust…you know?"

"Betsy didn't say anything about Carol staying with Ily the night before?" Thomas asked.

"Well, she mentioned Ily keeping her for the night, but nothing about them in the storm. She just said Carol got caught in the storm and now she has…That she's sick. I wonder why she didn't tell me she was with Ily?"

"Maybe she didn't want you to think it was Ily's fault. Because it isn't her fault. She tried to get to shelter before they got caught, but the storm was too fast for them," Thomas explained, feeling defensive of his wife.

"Yeah, you're probably right. But that's my baby girl."

"I know! But think of Ily and how she feels. She feels horrible, and it sounds like she's blaming herself. She thinks even Betsy blames her." Thomas looked down as Eddie shook his head.

"Do you know why Carol stayed at your place? Does Ily say?" Eddie asked quietly.

"She wanted to help out and try to keep Carol from asking where you are."

"Carol is always so curious about everything," Eddie sighed. "She wants to know how everything works."

"Hey," Billy interjected, making his presence known. "It says in the newspaper that the head recruiters have heard about the dust storm and want to help. And they said that if any of the draftees have a member of their family who's sick or injured, they'll be allowed to go home to tend to them. But only if the sickness is serious enough."

"What? Are you sure?" Thomas asked.

"Yeah, it's right here." Billy threw him the paper.

Thomas read it eagerly. "Well, imagine that, right there in black and white. Ed, you could be sent home to your baby girl. It says to talk to your sergeant."

Eddie just stood there, speechless.

"Well, what are you waiting for?" Thomas encouraged.

Eddie hesitated. "I can't just leave you guys," he said half-heartedly.

"Are you crazy? Of course you can. Listen, Eddie, that's your daughter. Your baby. Go home and fight this sickness with her, your wife, and your other children. They need your support. Especially Carol. She needs her strong father right beside her. Do you know what she's doing right now?"

Eddie shook his head.

"She's crying, and you know who for? You! She wants her daddy. Now go and march straight up to Sergeant Dow and Swoop, and demand they send you home to your crying baby girl."

With that, Eddie stood, saluted Thomas, and marched out the door.

A few minutes later, while Thomas and Billy were continuing to discuss the dust storm, Eddie walked back in. They noticed him and rushed over.

"What'd they say?" Thomas asked.

Eddie looked up at them with joy in his eyes. "I'm going home, boys. I'm going home to see my baby girl."

The following day, the sergeants sent a group of about thirty men back home to care for their ailing loved ones. Eddie was among them. He gave Thomas a hearty bear hug, then turned to Billy, ruffling his hair.

"You two stay safe and look out for each other," Eddie said.

"We will," Thomas assured him. "Give Ily a hug and a kiss from me—and to Betsy and Carol, too."

"I promise," Eddie replied.

"Take care of your little ones!" Thomas called after him, his voice thick with emotion. He wiped his damp eyes as Eddie climbed onto the truck, which rumbled to life and began pulling away.

5

ILY

Ily stepped up to Betsy's door. She raised her hand to knock but paused midair. She wasn't sure what she would say once she was face-to-face with Betsy. After a moment's hesitation, she knocked softly on the wooden door, waiting only a few seconds before deciding to turn and leave. She assumed Betsy wouldn't want to talk to her, anyway. But just as Ily began to walk away, the door suddenly flew open and Betsy ran out. She collapsed into Ily's arms and began to sob against her shoulder.

Together, they walked wordlessly into Betsy and Eddie's room, and Betsy resumed her previous position, kneeling beside Carol's bed.

"How is she today? Any changes?" Ily asked quietly, watching Betsy rub her ever-expanding belly.

Betsy didn't lift her eyes off the sleeping child as she softly shook her head.

"No."

"I was reading the newspaper, and there was a part about the war," Ily said. "It says that if any of the troops have loved ones that are sick from the storm, they may be sent home."

Betsy perked up. "Oh, Ily, do you think the boys will be sent home?"

"Maybe Eddie, but I don't think Thomas will," Ily said somberly.

Betsy stared at Ily in confusion. "Why not? Are you not sick? I just assumed, since you went to Dr. Rogers the other day. How do you feel?"

"Oh, I'm fine," Ily said hesitantly.

"So, what did the doctor say?"

"He just said that I'm healthy. And so is…my baby."

"Your baby?" Betsy gasped. "Are you pregnant?"

"Yes, and I've wanted to tell you ever since I found out, but I didn't know how to tell you with Carol being so ill." Ily's eyes filled with tears, relieved that she could finally confide in her best friend.

"Oh Ily, I would have understood," Betsy said softly. "We care about you so much. I'm so happy for you, and I want you to know I don't blame you for Carol being sick at all. You couldn't have known the dust storm was coming."

Betsy looked down at Carol and reached for her tiny hand, which burned from her fever.

"She'll get better," she sighed.

A few days later, Dr. Rogers made a house call to check on Carol. The ice wasn't relieving her fever at all. The little angel continued to spit up brown, gooey mucus in between her frequent slumbers.

The doctor was checking Carol's lungs when Betsy's eldest son, Noah, came rushing into the room.

"Mama!"

Both Betsy and Ily jumped up.

"What is it, Noah?" Betsy asked.

"There's a big dust storm headed our way."

"Oh, no, not again! Noah, where are the children?" Betsy asked frantically.

"Charles is in the barn tending to the doc's horse, Mary's in here, Joan and Carrie are in their rooms," Noah rattled off.

"Okay, quickly, get Charles and make sure all the doors are latched. Mary, bring Joan and Carrie in here," Betsy ordered as Noah ran out of the door and Mary rushed to collect her sisters.

Betsy hurried to the window to jimmy the board in place. The children ran in and slammed the door shut, and Betsy stuffed her quilt under it.

There was a stream of light peeking through a crack in the window, but it disappeared suddenly.

They all sat around Carol's bed, waiting for the storm to pass, listening to the wind howling and the grains of sand pelting into the side of the house. They all jumped at the sound of a huge bang coming from outside.

"What was that?" Ily yelped, reaching for Betsy's hand as the twin girls whimpered.

"I don't know," Betsy answered shakily.

Three more bangs were heard until Betsy realized that it was coming from the front door.

"Who could that be?"

Betsy slowly moved the quilt and opened the bedroom door, warning everyone to stay put. She made her way to the front door, covering her mouth with her dress skirt.

She struggled to open the door against the treacherous weather. She screamed as she recognized the dust-covered figure. Eddie rushed in and helped push the door closed, then ushered his wife back to the bedroom. The children jumped up when they saw their father and ran to him as he replaced the quilt.

Eddie embraced his family.

"I've missed you all so much. How's Carol?" He turned towards the bed and took in the sight of his weak little girl.

"Not good," Dr. Rogers answered quietly. "She wakes up every now and then, but she falls back asleep soon after, exhausted from coughing up more and more dust." He looked down at his feet to hide his tears.

Eddie kneeled by Carol's side. "Hey, baby girl," he whispered.

He twisted her curls around his finger and leaned down to gently kiss her cheek. He noticed her slow breathing and kept an eye on her chest to make sure it was still rising and falling. Carol coughed, and a tear rolled down Eddie's cheek.

"Daddy?" Carol's voice was barely a whisper.

Eddie glanced quickly at Betsy before looking back at Carol. Betsy knelt down beside them.

"Yes, sweetheart, Daddy's here. Mommy and Daddy are both here," Eddie reassured her.

Carol coughed, choking as she spat out brown mucus into the cloth that Betsy held gently under her chin.

"Daddy, I miss you," Carol said weakly.

Dr. Rogers walked over to Carol's bed to check her temperature and listen to her lungs again.

"That's the first time she's spoken in days," Betsy said.

"That could be a good sign," Dr. Rogers replied.

Eddie and Betsy embraced, clinging to the hopeful news.

6

THOMAS

"Alright, men, we didn't come this far to quit now," Sergeant Dow boomed. "Today, we're going to see what you daisies have learned over the last eight weeks, and then we'll get you ready for your final ceremony. Today, y'all are gonna march, run, jump, and shoot."

The day began with an early morning march and run before breakfast. Afterward, the men spent hours practicing navigation and shooting drills, refining their skills with precision. Following dinner, they continued honing their techniques, tackling more of the obstacle course as the sun began to set. By the time the day was over, exhaustion had overtaken them, and they fell asleep long before lights-out.

Ceremony Day arrived soon after, and the men were excited and ready to go. They stood at attention, waiting for the sergeants, who were quietly discussing amongst themselves. Dow looked up and noticed the draftees watching them, trying to eavesdrop. He cleared his throat.

"Now, one by one, y'all will show us what skills you've picked up during your time here. Then, when you're finished, we'll tell you who has passed and who will need more training."

"I volunteer to go first, Sergeant Dow, sir," Kelly said eagerly.

Sergeant Swoop rolled his eyes.

"Private Kelly, it seems you need more training in communication. Only speak when spoken to. But since you're itching like a snake in the grass, you may go first when it's time to start. Now, Sergeant Swoop's group will start with the obstacle course, and my group will start with navigation and gun routine."

Swoop and Dow led their respective groups. Dow stopped in front of the open field, where the men could see a line of dummies in the distance.

"We'll see if y'all can shoot a man from fifty yards away."

Dow raised his pistol, aimed at his target, and took his shot. The draftees marched towards the dummy, their curiosity piqued. They looked at the dummy in awe, poking their fingers through the hole where its heart would have been.

"Private Kelly, you may shoot first," Dow announced. "But before you shoot, you must assemble the rifle. After you've taken your shot, disassemble the rifle for the next man."

Kelly stepped forward and began assembling. He put the rifle together in half a minute, aimed, shot, and broke the weapon back down. Dow made his notes, walked over to inspect the dummy that had taken Kelly's shot, and returned to finish his brief notes.

"Alright, who's next?"

Jack, Kelly's right-hand man, volunteered after Kelly shot him a cold glare. Jack also assembled the rifle in half a minute and made his mark close to the heart. He took better aim than Kelly but took care not to make a point of it.

Dow then began calling names. Each man assembled and disassembled at different speeds, but their aims were mostly true and close to the dummies' hearts. A few men were a little shakier than others but still managed to hit near the head or the gut.

Billy was called next and stepped forward, clearly nervous. He wasn't fond of performing in front of large crowds; it always made it harder to focus. Taking a deep breath, he approached the table, grabbed the gun parts, and began piecing them together. Despite his nerves, he felt confident; he'd assembled the rifle countless times before during his training. He secured the base and barrel, positioned the trigger correctly, and finally felt everything click smoothly into place.

As he raised the rifle, he tried to control his shaking. He closed one eye and took a deep breath. He knew he'd be off target but took the shot anyway. He pulled the trigger, imagining his target.

BANG!

He opened his eyes and waited for the sergeant to return.

Billy almost missed Dow's smile—a rare sight. He had to look twice to believe it.

"Kid," Dow said, "you may be the shakiest gunman I've ever seen— but damn, you're the only one so far to hit the target exactly where I did. Good job."

Billy couldn't help but smile as he disassembled the rifle faster than he'd put it together.

Thomas's turn came, second to last. His assembly took one minute, and in that time, he realized how much he hated assembling and disassembling weapons. He knew how to do it, but the repetition wore him out. Still, he reminded himself that one day this skill could save his life. Taking aim, he confidently shot and waited as Dow walked down the field.

"Private Milton, are you alright? You must be having an off day. You shot the decoy right in its left eye," Sergeant Dow laughed. "Were you aiming at all?"

"Not for the eye, sir, no."

Thomas disassembled the rifle and waited as the last draftee stepped up.

The final recruit was short, skinny, and looked a little too old to be a draftee. He had always kept to himself and was very quiet. No one really knew him or could get him to share much about himself. But they just knew he wasn't really the war type. On their first night, as they all began to drift off after a long day of marching, they could hear him crying. They assumed he was crying for his family. The next day,

Thomas asked if he was alright and offered a few encouraging words. The man just kept his head down and kept walking, ignoring Thomas.

"Private Jones," Sergeant Dow boomed.

Jones stepped up, assembled the rifle faster than any of the other men had, took his shot, then disassembled it without waiting for Dow to check his mark. Dow walked down and searched for the bullet hole but found no new wound on the dummy.

With Jones being the last shooter, Dow dismissed them to the mess tent for lunch and much-needed coffee.

After lunch, Dow collected his group again to move on to the navigation drill. He announced that they would need to demonstrate what they had learned about how to navigate using the sun, moon, stars, and their compasses. The group was able to find their directions and locate the stars in their places, and everyone passed.

With all drills and testing completed for the day, they marched back and stood at attention by the ends of their bunks, just as they had begun their day. They listened closely to Sergeant Dow and Sergeant Swoop, all anxious to find out if they had passed.

Billy leaned toward Thomas, daring to whisper, "I heard if you don't pass, you have to do boot camp all over again."

Thomas nodded in agreement.

"Settle down, settle down," Sergeant Dow yelled, startling Billy back to his proper stance. "I know y'all are anxious to learn if you passed or not, and I do have the final results. Now, there are about fifty of you in this bunk, so I'm going to tell you who didn't pass since there were only a couple. I'm sorry—you did all this work just to do it all over again."

Sergeant Dow pulled out a sheet and unfolded it. "Alright. First person who didn't make it…" He cleared his throat. "Private Jones."

The men stole a glance at Jones. A brief sigh of relief flickered across his face before his expression quickly shifted to feigned shock.

"Private Lee," Sergeant Dow continued, then named ten more draftees.

Thomas and Billy felt grateful; they were among those who had passed, along with Jack and Kelly. Some of the other men who had passed were friendly with Thomas, while others were still strangers to him.

"Alright, those who weren't on my list, pack right away. We leave at o' seven hundred. There's a long trip ahead, waiting for us to march it. The rest of you, meet Sergeant Swoop in front of the mess hall. He will explain what will be expected of you next."

Thomas turned to his bunk and decided to write a quick letter to Ily about his last day, letting her know that he would soon be traveling to the front. Then he began packing his belongings.

The next morning, the men rose early, anxious to head out. This was what they had worked hard to prepare for, and they were ready.

"You alright, kid?" Thomas noticed Billy staring at his bunk.

"Yeah. It's just…this was my first bed to myself. I've never had my own before. I always either had to share or sleep on the floor."

They piled into the back of trucks with their duffle bags. They had only packed the essentials, including their uniforms and rifles. Once all the men were accounted for, they began their long journey toward danger at the front lines.

Sergeant Dow informed the group that it would take about three days to reach the base camp in Frankfort, Kentucky.

"So, a lot of time to think, especially about the dangers along the way," he said, keeping them alert.

Thomas felt ready to begin his new adventure.

7

ILY

Ily was woken from a deep sleep by a knock on the door. As she pulled on her robe, she noticed it was still dark outside.

"Who could be out this late?" she wondered aloud.

She opened the door and saw a tall young man wearing an Army uniform, his mop of hair slightly disheveled.

"May I help you?" Ily asked.

"Ma'am, you don't know me, but I knew your husband," the young man said.

"Do you work for the Army?"

"Yes. My name is Billy. I'm sorry to tell you, but your husband is dead."

Ily shot up and screamed, only to calm herself as she realized that it had only been a horrible nightmare.

Ily knocked on Betsy's door, and Eddie greeted her with a smile. Her eyes immediately welled up.

"Are you alright, Ily?" Eddie asked.

Ily slowly nodded and cleared her throat, croaking out a question about Carol's health.

"Oh, much better," Betsy announced as she walked up and grabbed Ily in a bear hug, cutting Eddie off before he could answer. "Her mucus is still yellow, but the doctor said she's going to be okay."

They walked into Carol's room and noticed her laughing with her siblings.

"This is the first time any of us have heard her laugh in weeks," Betsy said, keeping her gaze on her happy children.

"Hi, Aunt Ily!" Carol said excitedly.

"Oh, Carol!" Ily hurried over and lifted her, holding her tightly. "You feeling okay?"

"Oh, much better," Carol cheered.

"I brought you some daisies. I know they're your favorite," Ily said, setting Carol down and bending to her level to pass her the delicate flowers.

"Oh, thank you, Auntie. They're beautiful."

Carol stuck one into her red hair. She loved putting wild daisies in her hair and enjoying their sweet fragrance.

"I'm so glad you taught me how to make them stay in my hair, Auntie! I love you!"

Ily laughed, knowing Carol was starting to feel like her old self again.

"Mommy, can I sit outside?" Carol asked, turning to Betsy.

"I don't know," Betsy hesitated.

"Well, I don't see why not," Eddie interjected.

"Maybe she shouldn't," Betsy said worriedly.

"Why not, Betsy?"

"It could make her sick again. I don't want her relapsing."

"She won't," Eddie reassured her. "And besides, fresh air will do her good."

He had already picked Carol up and was heading out the door. Betsy stayed close on his heels.

Following the rest of the children outside, Ily heard Carol ask her father, "Is this what fresh air smells like?"

"Sure is, babe," Eddie answered, sitting down next to her.

Eddie and Carol watched the children chase their ball back and forth, while Ily and Betsy sat together on the front porch.

"How are you feeling now, Mama?" Betsy asked, watching Ily's stomach.

"Good. Not feeling much yet, being only a month along. I just get really nauseated in the mornings. I feel like I need to vomit, but nothing ever comes up."

"Yeah, I'm happy I don't have morning sickness anymore. That's probably the worst thing when you're pregnant, but everything is worth it when you see your baby," Betsy said, rubbing her tummy. "Yup, he'll be here soon—in about a month."

"How do you know it's a boy?"

"I can feel it. He moves a lot. I'll be happy when he meets all his siblings." Betsy smiled, thinking about how her life was about to change.

Ily smiled too but soon remembered her nightmare. Betsy noticed her frowning.

"You okay?"

"I'm alright. Along with this pregnancy, I also have terrible dreams. My dream of Thomas keeps replaying in my head—more like a nightmare. I just have a feeling, Betsy…that I won't see him again. I want my Thomas back." A tear rolled down her cheek.

"I'm so sorry," Betsy said, feeling a wave of guilt, knowing that her husband was back while Ily's wasn't.

It wasn't long before they noticed the children running up to the porch.

"What's going…?" Betsy stopped mid-sentence as she felt a sudden change in the wind and noticed dust blowing off the roof.

"Eddie, get Carol inside!" Betsy screamed.

Eddie stood to pick up the startled Carol as dust began to cover the porch. He pushed her face into his chest, rushing inside after the other children, with the women following. Together, they all forced the door shut.

They were all silent as they listened to yet another storm blow above. Ily and Betsy rushed to stuff rags into the cracks in the doors and windows. Ever since Black Sunday, they couldn't help but feel nervous whenever another dust storm came. They always counted their blessings when the storms didn't last long.

"I'm so sorry, baby girl," Eddie said as he held Carol.

"It's okay," Carol coughed. "But I don't feel good."

"Oh no," Betsy said, grabbing her and carrying her back to her little bed.

"Mommy, I can't breathe."

"Eddie, she's burning up again," Betsy said, wringing her hands.

Eddie rushed in. "It's all my fault," he cried.

"No, Eddie, it's not," Betsy argued.

"Mommy, I can't..." Carol choked out before coughing again, spitting out thick saliva.

"We need Dr. Rogers," Betsy said to Eddie.

"But we can't get him. Look outside," Ily said, pointing to the window. It was as dark as the night sky.

"I'll go," Eddie volunteered.

"No, you can't! I won't allow it," Betsy argued.

"Betsy, do we have a choice? Carol needs medicine."

"I just got you back. I don't want to lose you again."

"You won't, I promise. I'm going. I'll be right back with help."

Eddie had made up his mind. He turned to Carol.

"Baby, you hang in there. Daddy will be right back."

Betsy stopped him at the front door.

"Please, Eddie, don't go. It won't last long. Let's just wait it out."

"And if it doesn't stop soon? What do we do then? Keep waiting? What would you have done if I hadn't come home?" Eddie demanded. "What would have happened if the Army hadn't sent me home? *What would you have done?*"

Betsy stared at him, speechless.

"What if she gets worse while we wait?" Eddie continued. "What if she…"

He stopped himself, unable to say the words aloud. He didn't want to think about what could happen.

"I'm going," he said sternly.

He wrapped his head with the two wet towels that Ily had prepared for him—one to catch the dust and one to filter the air. He put on snow goggles to protect his eyes, then turned toward the women and children.

"I'll be back with the doctor."

He opened the door and was gone.

8

EDDIE

As soon as Eddie stepped out of the door, dust covered him. He couldn't even hear the door shutting behind him, and his vision turned dark immediately. Reaching out his hand, he found the stair rail. As he descended the steps, he fell to the ground on his belly, deciding that crawling would be easier.

He kept wiping the piling dust from his goggles. He had a long way to go to reach town, but he tried to remember the path and prayed he was still headed in the right direction. The wind and dust pushed him around and he struggled to crawl in a straight line. He could barely see his outstretched hands as he felt around for obstacles. He regretted that he hadn't thought to wear gloves to protect his hands against the wind and whipping sand. Despite the difficulty, he continued crawling as straight as he could.

Suddenly, his hand hit something solid. Feeling the roughness of wood, he realized it was a door. He pulled himself up to stand and, with the help of the wind, pushed the door open. He stumbled into a small room and wiped his goggles, recognizing the abandoned shed—the same one in which Ily and Carol had been trapped during the fateful Black Blizzard. Pushing the door closed, he watched dust begin to settle on the floor of the shed.

Eddie sat down to rest and collect his bearings. He removed his goggles and towels, shaking out the dust and debris. The goggles had worked as best as they could, though they had required constant clearing. The towels were still damp in places, though the one covering his head was almost completely dry, albeit caked in mud. He was shocked but grateful for how well they had worked.

After a moment's rest, he decided to head back out. *Halfway there,* he told himself. Pushing the door open, he was immediately pounded by coarse dust that stung the uncovered parts of his face. He crouched low to the ground, arms outstretched, trying to waddle his way forward.

Eddie recalled the compass he had brought back from boot camp and pulled it from his pocket. Shielding it from the dust as best he could, he raised it to his eyes and saw it pointing northwest—the direction in which he needed to go.

He tried to keep walking but was pushed down by the wind. As he fell, the compass flew from his hand. He dropped to the ground and felt around blindly with his hands before giving up.

He forced himself to stay calm and calculate his next move. He decided to return to the shed and began crawling in what he hoped was the right direction. He prayed he hadn't strayed too far during his search for the compass.

Suddenly, his arm struck something solid, and he felt the wood of the shed wall once more. Tracing his hands along it, he found the corner and, finally, the door. He stood at the door, dropped back to the ground, and crawled in the direction of town.

His slow, steady crawl felt endless, but the wind began to ease, and the pounding of dust against him subsided. He could feel the storm letting up. He stood up slowly and found that the wind was still strong but not as forceful. He thanked the Lord and staggered forward.

As he walked, keeping his face down and arms crossed over his head, the sun began to peek through the dust. He lowered his arms and could hardly believe his eyes as the dust settled and brick buildings came into view. He recognized the doctor's office, and he ran the rest of the way and shoved the door open.

"What in all the worlds is going on here?" Dr. Rogers gasped as Eddie ran into the waiting room. "Who are you, and what are you doing here?"

Eddie pulled off his head protection. "It's me, Eddie!" he exclaimed, panting.

"How did you find your way here in this chaos?" the doctor asked bewilderedly.

"For my daughter's health," Eddie replied.

"You're crazy, trying to get through a storm…"

"It's my daughter, Doc. She's sick again. We need your help," Eddie interrupted.

"And you expect me to go back with you?"

"Doc, my daughter needs you," Eddie pleaded, confused by the doctor's hesitation.

Dr. Rogers sighed.

"Eddie, I hoped I wouldn't have to tell you this, but…" He paused. "There's nothing more I can do for Carol. I'm so sorry."

"What?" Eddie froze.

"From her first diagnosis, I knew I couldn't help her. It was too late. Her little body can't overcome the dust in her lungs."

"I don't believe it. There must be something to help her get better." Eddie's voice broke, tears filling his eyes. "People get dust pneumonia all the time, and they recover."

"I know, Eddie," Dr. Rogers said gently. "But Carol is so little and delicate. The dust overtook her lungs, and they just aren't strong enough. Adults who survive can usually clear their lungs, but Carol's are too damaged."

"She got better once. She can get better again. Can't she?" Eddie asked desperately. "She got better until I stupidly let her go outside."

"If she recovers, it will be a miracle, just like the first time. But even if she hadn't gone outside, she still would have relapsed. Have you noticed, Eddie? She got better right when you returned home."

9

ILY

An hour or two later, the women noticed that the wind was beginning to die down.

"Where is he?" Betsy cried. "He should've been back by now. I knew this would happen. I shouldn't have let him go," she said, wringing her hands.

"Calm down. I'm sure Dr. Rogers told him to wait, and that she'll be alright," Ily replied soothingly.

"Sure, he won't listen to his wife, but he'll listen to a doctor," Betsy argued. "Oh, God, he's probably lying in a field unconscious. The storm's over—I should go look for him."

Just as Betsy started toward the door, it burst open. Eddie walked in, covered in dirt.

"Eddie!" Betsy ran to him, hugging him before stepping back and slapping him. "That's for giving me a fright!" She hugged him again.

She looked past him, expecting to see Dr. Rogers. "Where's the doctor?"

"Um…" Eddie looked at Betsy. The slap hadn't even fazed him. "I didn't get to see him," he sighed.

"What? So you risked your life for nothing?" Betsy asked.

"Yeah, can you believe that? At least I made it back safe."

The next day, as she walked back to the Ryesons' home, Ily noticed Eddie sitting on the porch. He stared off into space dejectedly, and didn't even acknowledge Ily's presence as she approached.

"Everything okay?"

He shook his head. "No."

"What's wrong? Is Carol okay?"

"Yes, she is…well, for now."

"Then what is it? Betsy? The baby?"

"No, it's not Betsy."

"Then what's bothering you? Wait, what do you mean, 'for now'?"

Eddie looked down.

"Eddie? What is it?"

"I lied."

"Lied about what?"

"I lied to Betsy. I never lie—especially to Betsy. She can always tell when someone's lying to her."

"What do you mean, you lied? What did you lie about?"

Eddie looked up at her. "I lied about not seeing Dr. Rogers. I did see him yesterday. I made it to town just as the storm was ending."

Ily's mouth hung open. "Why did you lie about that? What did he tell you? Aren't you the one who gave Betsy a long speech about doing everything possible to save Carol's life?"

"Yes, I was, but…" Eddie's voice trailed off as he looked back down.

"But what? Don't you want Carol to get better?"

"Of course I do, but…"

"But what? What are you not telling us?" Ily's frustration grew.

"He's a fraud," Eddie said angrily, standing up.

"Eddie? What did he say?"

"He said there's no hope for her." Eddie swallowed hard. "How am I supposed to admit that to Betsy—or to my little girl?"

He collapsed back onto the porch stairs and began to sob.

"Especially when she's crying in pain or can't breathe... and I know there's nothing I can do for her."

"Oh, Eddie, I'm so sorry." Ily sat down beside him, wrapping her arm around him.

"What do we do now? Just sit back and let her suffer?" Eddie said.

"No, of course not."

"What do I tell Betsy?" he repeated desperately.

"The truth."

"About yesterday?"

Ily nodded. "About everything."

Just then, Betsy came outside. Eddie and Ily jumped up from the porch stairs.

"Oh good, you're here," Betsy said, but her smile quickly faded when she noticed their serious expressions.

"What's going on?" She looked back and forth between them, stopping at Eddie. "Eddie, have you seen the doctor?"

Eddie looked up. "Um... no."

"What? Where could he be?"

"No, Betsy, what I mean is that I didn't see him today—but yesterday I did."

"What? I don't understand. You told us you didn't see him."

Betsy turned to Ily. "Ily, what is he talking about?"

Ily looked at Betsy and then at Eddie. "I think I should leave you two to talk," she said, heading inside.

Ily sat by Carol's bed, watching her sleep. It was quiet in the house. Noah and Charles were working in the fields, and Mary, Joan, and Carrie were at school. Carol looked peaceful, except for the occasional cough as she slept.

As Ily prayed, she realized how precious life was and how quickly it could end. She thought of Thomas and the other soldiers risking their lives in war. She was so lost in her thoughts that she didn't notice Betsy until she saw her sliding into bed next to Carol, wrapping her arms around her precious baby girl.

"I'm so sorry, baby," Betsy whispered in Carol's ear.

"No," Carol grunted. "PLEASE GET OFF. IT HURTS. PLEASE GET OFF. DON'T TOUCH ME!" she screamed.

Ily jumped forward in her chair. Betsy jumped back.

"What's going on?" Eddie said, running into the room.

Betsy stood there, shocked. "I don't know. I just laid down, and she started screaming for me to get off. She said it hurts."

"Mommy, I'm freezing," Carol said. "Where's my blanket? Mommy, my blankie! I want my blankie!"

All three of them stared at the pink quilted blanket already covering Carol's small body.

Betsy leaned forward, trying to comfort her daughter. "Sweetie, you have your blanket. It's on you right now."

"No, Mommy, no, it's not. I'm so cold," Carol begged, her teeth beginning to chatter. "I'm so tired, but I don't want to lie down. Can I sit in Daddy's chair? Please!"

"I don't know. I think you'd be more comfortable in your nice, warm bed," Betsy said, kissing her forehead before looking at Eddie.

"It might make her warmer to be bundled up in the chair rather than stretched out," Eddie suggested, moving closer to the bed. "Okay, sweetie, I'm going to lift you up, okay?"

"No, don't, Daddy. I hurt all over. Let me walk."

"Do you think you can?" Eddie asked, taking a deep breath.

Carol stayed still for a moment, gathering her strength. Slowly, she moved her foot to the edge of the bed and lowered it to the floor. As she tried lifting herself off the bed, she immediately shrieked in pain, the agony shooting up to her head.

Betsy rushed forward to catch and comfort her daughter.

"Oww!" Carol wailed, falling back onto the bed.

"What happened?" Eddie asked, dumbfounded.

"My foot—it hurts. My whole body hurts," Carol cried.

Betsy tried to comfort her and encouraged her to stay in bed.

"No, I want to try again. I'm tired of this bed," Carol panted.

She moved her foot closer to the edge of the bed and lowered it once more, gritting her teeth. She managed one step forward, still gripping the edge of the bed, but on her second step, she began to fall. Eddie caught her and picked her up, heading towards the armchair.

"Daddy, no. It's too painful. Please put me down," Carol begged.

Eddie gently placed her in his overstuffed armchair, tucking her blanket around her and plumping a pillow for her head.

"Blankie? My blankie?" Carol repeated.

"Shh, sweetie. It's right here!" Eddie cooed.

"No! I don't want to lie down. Please, I'm so cold."

"Oh, Eddie, she's not making any sense," Betsy said with tears in her eyes.

"I'm going to get Dr. Rogers," Ily said, moving toward the door.

Eddie grabbed her arm. "He won't come. There's nothing we can do," he said, his voice trembling as tears filled his eyes.

"Well, maybe he can at least put our minds at ease and tell us what's wrong—why she's not making any sense!" Ily argued.

Eddie slowly released her arm and nodded in agreement.

"Ily told me what's going on," Dr. Rogers said as he entered, with Ily at his heels. "I believe Carol is going into septic shock, which could mean a couple of things."

"Like what?" Eddie asked, jumping up. He and Betsy had been sitting on either side of Carol while she continued to sleep in the armchair.

"Well, it could mean low blood pressure, an infection settling into her body, or…" Dr. Rogers paused.

"Or what? Almanzo!" Betsy demanded, her tone stern.

"Or organ failure."

Betsy gasped. "No." She looked down at Carol, tears clouding her vision. "Not my baby."

"It's my fault," Eddie said anxiously. "I'm the one who took her out when we knew she shouldn't go. She seemed to be getting better."

"Eddie, that doesn't matter," Dr. Rogers said. "She would've fallen weak again even if you hadn't taken her out. It's how the disease works, I'm afraid."

"This is all my fault," Ily whimpered.

Betsy turned to her.

"No, Ily. Don't you dare think like that. You didn't know. How could you have known?"

Ily looked at Betsy woefully.

"I didn't know when we left my house. But when we got to the top of the hill, I saw the wall of dust."

She looked away.

"I thought we could make it to you before it hit, but we only got halfway before it blocked our view of your house. So we ran back to the shed, but when we reached it, the cloud had already gotten to us. I'm so sorry. I tried my hardest to keep her safe."

Ily stopped, trying to control her sobbing.

"Ily, you need to calm yourself and avoid this stress—it could hurt your baby!" Dr. Rogers said firmly.

"Please forgive me," Ily continued, still staring at Betsy. "I understand if you can't. I know I'll never forgive myself."

Ily stood and headed to the door.

"Ily, wait," Betsy called. "Please don't go."

Ily stopped, facing the door. "We should have just turned around and run to the shed. Carol would be at school right now with her sisters." She opened the door and walked out without looking back.

Betsy did her best to reach the door, but her baby bump slowed her down and she could only waddle after Ily. She stopped on the porch and watched as Ily disappeared over the hill.

"I do forgive you!" she called after Ily.

Betsy walked back inside and noticed Dr. Rogers standing over Carol.

"What's happening, Eddie?" she asked.

Eddie moved closer to Betsy without a word, and she repeated, more insistently, "What's going on?"

"She's having a seizure!" Dr. Rogers shouted, trying to hold Carol down.

Betsy rushed to his side and saw Carol's eyes rolling back into her head. She turned away, sobbing, terrified by Carol's convulsions.

"No, no, not my baby!" she screamed.

"Eddie, get her out of here!" Dr. Rogers ordered.

Eddie turned his eyes away from his daughter and grabbed Betsy by the shoulders, dragging her toward the door.

"Betsy, I know this is hard, but the doctor is doing everything he can to help her. We can't get in his way," Eddie insisted, struggling to haul her out of the room.

"I am *not* in the way! That is my daughter. Don't you dare pull me away, Edward!"

Betsy twisted free of his grasp and rushed back to Carol's side.

Carol's spasms had slowed, and Dr. Rogers carefully straightened her in the armchair to make her more comfortable.

"She seems calm now," he said. "But be prepared—she could have another seizure at any time."

He turned to his supplies and pulled out a device with a small bag attached to tubing and a nosepiece.

"This is an oxygen mask. It will help her breathe, especially after a seizure. It won't hurt to keep it on her; it'll support her little lungs. This seizure seemed minor, and hopefully, any future ones will be, too."

"Mommy?" Carol spoke weakly, her face tightening with pain.

"It's okay, baby. Mommy's here. What's wrong?" Betsy asked, trying to stay calm.

"Mommy, it..." Carol grunted, clutching her chest. "It hurts. My chest. It hurts really, really bad. Daddy, make it stop."

"Can you explain how and where it hurts?" Dr. Rogers asked gently.

"All over!" Carol grunted. "Like someone's hugging me really hard—and they're on fire. It's hard to breathe."

"Doctor, look at her skin—it's gray," Eddie said, pulling Betsy closer.

"Carol, you're going to be okay," Dr. Rogers said. "I need you to relax and breathe very slowly—in through your nose and out through your mouth. I'm going to put this mask over your face. It will help you breathe. Slow breaths, okay?" He soothed her as he secured the mask over her face.

He listened to her chest with his stethoscope. "Slow, calm breaths, Carol," he repeated, his voice steady. He closed his eyes as he listened.

"I hear rattling in her lungs. I do have some medicine, but in her condition, it's not going to help much."

Carol's breathing gradually slowed, and she relaxed enough to drift back to sleep.

"I wish I could make it all go away," Dr. Rogers said mournfully, closing his doctor's bag.

1 0

BETSY

Ily was in the middle of reading Thomas's latest letter when she heard a knock on her door. To her surprise, she opened it to find Betsy standing there.

"Hello," Ily greeted quietly.

"Hey, how are you feeling?"

"Okay. How's Carol?"

"Not good."

Ily felt hot tears rolling down her cheek. She turned away to hide them.

"Ily, don't cry, please. It's not your fault."

"But it is, Betsy. It is!"

"No, it's not," Betsy replied sternly. "Now, stop saying that. No one blames you. Not Eddie, me, Carol, or any of the kids. You did your best; you did what you had to. I would have done the same thing. Please don't cry," she begged as she embraced Ily.

"I'm so sorry," Ily bawled on Betsy's shoulder.

"Shh." Betsy patted her back. "Calm down. Remember what the doctor said: you shouldn't have all this stress. Trust me, I know! Will you come back with me? Carol needs her whole family beside her, including her cousin."

Betsy grinned, and Ily returned it faintly.

"There's that beautiful smile," Betsy said.

Ily kneeled beside Carol's bed, holding onto her doll-like hand. Carol was sleeping peacefully. Her skin was pale, almost colorless, and her little almond-shaped eyes were sunken in and framed by dark circles.

"I'm so sorry, baby girl," Ily whispered.

Carol's eyes flew open. "Where's Uncle Tommy?"

Ily looked at Carol with wide eyes. "He's, um…He's not here, sweetie. Remember, he went with your daddy out of town."

"Yes, but Daddy came back. Why didn't Uncle Tommy come with him?"

Ily tried to think of how best to explain. "Well, because I wasn't sick, sweetie. Your daddy heard you were sick and wanted to be home to care for you. Uncle Tommy loves you and misses you dearly. In fact, he wrote to me that he is sending you a teddy bear in the mail."

Tears welled in Ily's eyes.

"I don't need anything, Auntie," Carol said. "All I want is my family."

"Uncle Tommy also said that this bear has magical powers," Ily continued. "Whenever you hug the bear, it'll feel like you're hugging Uncle Tommy, and you'll feel all better."

She couldn't contain herself any longer; her tears broke free. Eddie walked into the room and saw Carol and Ily crying together.

"Woah, what happened here?"

"Daddy, Auntie said Uncle Tommy is sending me a magic bear that will make me all better," Carol said, wiping her eyes.

"That's nice of Uncle Tommy." Eddie smiled and looked towards Ily. She nodded back and smiled at Carol.

They all spent the rest of the day granting Carol's wish by surrounding her with their presence. As Betsy sat beside Carol, holding her hand, she realized that her whole family was finally together. For a moment, their worries were gone, and they were all enjoying themselves. The children laughed as Eddie told them a story. Betsy savored the sound. For the first time in what had felt like forever, love and joy filled the room instead of cries. She grinned at all the smiles around the room. She clung to the moment, unwilling to let reality steal it away.

Then Betsy stopped smiling. Her chest tightened. Something felt terribly wrong. Time slowed as she became lost in thought. The sounds of laughter became muffled, as if she were underwater. Suddenly, she realized that the laughter was all she had been hearing. Her heart dropped as she realized that had stopped hearing Carol's occasional coughing.

Betsy's heart sank as she looked down and watched Carol take her final breath.

Carol's burial service was held two days later. Everyone close to the family came to offer their condolences and say their final goodbyes to Carol Viola Ryeson.

Ily walked up to hug Betsy, Eddie, and their children.

"This just arrived yesterday in the mail," she said. "It's the teddy bear Thomas sent. He also included a letter saying how sorry he is for not being here." She handed the bear to Besty, who pulled her in for another hug.

"Thank you," said Betsy. "This would have meant the world to her—especially knowing it came from Uncle Tommy."

She walked over to Carol's open casket and gently placed the bear in the girl's arms.

"There. Now it will always be with her."

She stood there for a moment, remembering Carol's smiles and giggles.

Carol lay peacefully in her tiny casket, her hands placed neatly across her stomach. Her red, curly hair was pinned back with a white daisy behind one ear, the rest framing her petite face. She was wearing her favorite dress, adorned with little embroidered daisies.

"Doesn't she look so peaceful just lying there?" Betsy asked Eddie as he walked up.

"Yes, she sure does," he replied.

"Like she's just sleeping and will wake up as soon as she smells pancakes and syrup warming on the stove."

"Those were her favorite. I feel the same way," Eddie said. "She's in a better place now. She isn't suffering anymore. I bet she's up there now, watching over us—when she's not playing or picking daisies. She's in a better place." His voice broke as tears streamed down his face.

They walked back to join Ily and their children as Carol's casket was lowered into the ground.

As people began to leave the gravesite, Ily saw Betsy suddenly clutch her stomach and nearly collapse. Eddie caught her just in time. Ily ran over to help.

"Are you okay?" Ily asked.

"Yes, but—" Betsy turned to Eddie, her face strained. "I think our baby is coming!"

"Are you sure?" Eddie asked, his voice tinged with excitement.

"Yes!" Betsy screamed, clutching her stomach tighter.

"Will you help me lift her into the truck?" Eddie asked Ily.

Ily nodded, and together they each took an arm and helped Betsy into the bed of the truck. Eddie climbed in with Betsy as Ily drove them into town to Dr. Rogers' office.

"Almanzo? Almanzo!" Ily shouted as she and Eddie guided Betsy toward the front door of the office.

"What's the matter?" Dr. Rogers asked, stepping out to meet them.

"The baby—it's coming!" Eddie announced.

Dr. Rogers quickly took charge, helping Eddie guide Betsy into the examination room. Ily stayed outside to watch over the children.

"Watch your step. Here, Betsy, lie down," Dr. Rogers said as he and Eddie gently helped her onto the exam table.

"Thank you," Betsy managed to say before another scream of pain escaped her lips.

"Alright, let's calm down a bit," Dr. Rogers said soothingly as he prepared towels and blankets. "Breathe slowly, Betsy. Inhale through your nose and exhale through your mouth. Everything will be fine, I promise. Here."

He took Eddie's hand and placed it in Betsy's.

"Squeeze his hand if you need to."

Dr. Rogers bent down to listen for the baby's heartbeat. "Sounds like the baby's in the right position to push," he said, looking up at Betsy. "Are you ready?"

Betsy nodded. "Get him out!"

Eddie laughed. "Still holding onto those dreams of yours? Well, you've been right every time, to be fair."

Dr. Rogers pulled a stool up to the end of the table and propped Betsy's legs up. He immediately noticed the baby's head beginning to crown.

"Alright, Mama, I can see your baby. Now get ready to push."

Betsy gritted her teeth and screamed as she pushed with all her might.

"Breathe slowly—inhale through your nose and exhale through your mouth," Dr. Rogers coached. "You're doing great, Betsy. Keep going. Just one more push!"

With a final yell, Betsy gave one last push. A tiny whimper quickly grew into a high-pitched cry.

"Congratulations—it's a boy!" Dr. Rogers exclaimed, holding the newborn up for Betsy and Eddie to see.

Eddie, stunned that Betsy was right once again, kissed her forehead. "I love you," he whispered.

Betsy let her pinned-up hair fall loose. Beads of sweat dripped down her cheeks as she smiled at her husband.

Dr. Rogers cleaned up the baby and handed him to Betsy.

"Hello, little one," Betsy said softly, cradling him in her arms. Ily brought the children inside one by one to meet their new sibling.

"What's his name, Mama?" Joan asked eagerly.

Betsy glanced at Eddie and smiled.

"Carl," she said.

11

THOMAS

It was the second week of May when the soldiers left boot camp. The journey was a difficult one, and the weather did not make it any easier. On the first day of their journey, it poured relentlessly, well into the night.

The next day, the sun peeked out from between the parting clouds, and the men spent the day drying out their uniforms and equipment. Although the sun helped dry the items hanging on the clotheslines, it soon turned the rest of the day unbearably humid.

Finally, they arrived at the camp, where rows of tents, marked with large red-cross symbols, stood orderly. Men dressed in white rushed in and out of the tents while cries of excruciating pain echoed from every direction.

The trucks came to a stop to unload supplies, and the men came out to stretch their legs. Thomas and Billy wandered around with a few other soldiers while they waited.

As Thomas and Billy passed by one of the tents, they stopped and peeked inside. Thomas noticed Billy turn pale. Inside, men were being treated for gunshot and grenade wounds. Some were missing limbs. A man near the entrance lay stiff as a board, his head wrapped in blood-stained bandages.

"Is he...?" Billy asked, hesitant to finish the question.

"No," Thomas replied. "He's not dead."

Nearby, two wounded soldiers sat just outside another tent, bandages wrapped around various parts of their bodies. One of the men was trying to feel for a leg that wasn't there, his hand groping the empty space where the limb had been. Billy stared until the other soldier called out to him.

"Hey, kid! What're you staring at? Pretty soon, that's gonna be you!"

Billy turned toward the soldier, only to jump back in shock. The man had a bandage across his head, with a bloody circle marking where his right eye had once been.

Thomas quickly pulled Billy away.

"Don't listen to him, Billy"

"It's horrible to see them like that," Billy said, his voice shaking. "Kind of gets you thinking, doesn't it, Thomas?"

Thomas nodded, unable to shake the gruesome sights. He began to wonder what would happen if he were to end up like those men. It was then that he finally realized that war wasn't just about money. He remembered all the things that Ily had said the day he'd received his draft letter.

"Oh, Ily, you were right," Thomas murmured under his breath.

"You alright, Thomas?" Billy asked.

Thomas shook his head clear. "Yeah, all good."

"Thomas?" a voice called out.

Thomas turned around and saw a tall man with piercing green eyes and a blond buzz cut that made him look nearly bald.

"Thomas, right?" the man asked. "It's Jo! Remember? You and your friends gave your room to my group in Frankfurt."

"Jo?" Thomas paused, trying to place him. Then he recognized him. "Jo! It is you! Man, you look so different without all your hair and your mustache." Thomas shook his hand firmly.

Jo nodded at Billy before glancing around. "Where's your other friend?"

"Eddie? He got sent home. His little girl got caught in that storm everyone's calling Black Sunday, and now she's sick with dust pneumonia."

"Oh, man, I heard about that storm. That's terrible news. I hope she pulls through. That disease is the worst."

"Especially for Carol. She's only six," Thomas said, his voice heavy with emotion. "In my last letter, my wife said there are good days and bad days. I sent Carol a teddy bear to brighten her day and give her some hope."

"Only six? That's rough. I'll be praying for her. Be sure to keep me updated," Jo said.

"Will do," Thomas promised.

"Be ready to move out soon!" a soldier called from the trucks.

"I was wondering when we'd get to see some real action," Billy said eagerly. "Have you been to the front yet, Jo?"

"No, not yet," Jo replied. "Most of the men here have, though. The only reason they're at this camp is because they're too injured to fight anymore—or worse. If you end up here, it's because you've lost a limb or are otherwise unable to fight…or you're dead. A lot of men here need surgery. They say war changes you—makes you do crazy things. One man lost both his legs, and his friend said he went so crazy it drove him to his grave."

"That won't happen to me," Billy said defiantly. "I'm gonna make it back to my mama and my brother and sister. But if I don't, they'll know I did my very best and died a hero."

He glanced at Thomas for support.

"You okay, Tom? You've been quiet ever since we got to this camp. What's going on?"

Thomas stared into space until Billy tapped him on the shoulder.

"Huh? What?"

"You okay?"

"Oh, yeah, fine," Thomas said, though his thoughts remained on Ily.

Thomas, Billy, and Jo joined a group of about twelve men, standing at attention as General Hobbs and Colonel Nelson addressed them. Thomas recognized Kelly and Jack among the group. Hobbs explained that the journey ahead would take two days, and as they neared the front lines, they would be marching on foot. With the sun already setting, it was time to start moving.

After a few hours of marching, the group found a good spot to rest for the night. Thomas, Billy, and Jo settled against a large tree, each taking their own side as they tried to sleep.

Before they could fall into a deep sleep, a loud blast in the distance startled them.

"Was that thunder?" Billy asked.

Colonel Nelson chuckled. "No, no, don't fret. You'll get used to it," he replied. "Those are cannon blasts from the battlefield. Like I said, you'll get used to it—or you'd better, because you're going to be hearing that day and night."

The next morning, they rose before the sun to get an early start. They were still exhausted from the previous day's marching and the discomfort of sleeping on the ground. Some men shivered, shaking off the dew that had settled on them during the night.

"Alright, men, let's get moving before we're spotted. The closer we get to camp, the closer we get to enemy lines," General Hobbs warned.

The blasts and gunshots grew louder and more distinct with each step they took. The air seemed to grow foggier.

"We're close, men. Watch yourselves, stay low, and keep quiet," Hobbs instructed.

They remained crouched as they continued.

"Isn't this exciting?" Billy whispered.

Thomas and Jo exchanged glances before looking back at Billy.

Jo chuckled softly. "Eager boy you've got there, Tom."

The sound of gunshots and cannon blasts filled Thomas's ears, the smoke burning his nose. He felt his stomach churn. The reality of the situation began to set in, and he couldn't shake the feeling of dread that had settled into him.

They marched on until Hobbs raised his fist in the air.

"Halt!" he commanded. "Listen—did anyone hear that?"

Colonel Nelson scanned the trees, his eyes darting in all directions as he tried to pick up on what General Hobbs had heard.

"Men, steady yourselves for what might happen next," Hobbs continued. "Whatever does happen, remember—if you die, you die with honor."

The men loaded their rifles and aimed them southward toward the trees.

Thomas's ears began to ring as the world around him seemed to fall silent. He could only hear his own breath as he searched for movement in the trees.

Hobbs was about to call for the men to continue moving when the snap of a twig broke the stillness.

"Fire!" someone yelled, and they all opened fire at once.

"CEASE FIRE! CEASE FIRE! CEASE FIRE!" Nelson shouted over the thunderous explosions of black powder.

Slowly, the men stopped shooting but kept their rifles aimed at the woods. They stood motionless for what felt like an eternity, waiting for something to emerge. When nothing did, they cautiously began to march again. Moving in a single file, they stayed low and quiet, their boots crunching through dead leaves as they maneuvered around trees and bushes. Thomas walked behind Jo and Billy, while Kelly and Jack brought up the rear.

The silence was shattered by a sudden blast and a grunt from behind.

"Who opened fire?" Colonel Nelson demanded.

They all froze when they saw Jack collapse on top of Kelly, blood spreading across his back.

Nelson looked between Jack and the woods, then shouted, "AMBUSH! TAKE COVER AND OPEN FIRE!"

The men quickly reloaded their rifles and began firing into the trees.

Thomas spotted a thick patch of brush and pulled Billy and Jo behind it.

"Take cover!" Thomas shouted toward Kelly, who was still pinned beneath Jack. Kelly looked up at Thomas before shoving Jack off and grabbing his rifle. Tucking the weapon against his left arm, he dragged Jack toward the brush while keeping low.

"Keep firing, men!" a voice called out, barely audible over the chaos.

Thomas could hear Kelly whispering to Jack, urging him to stay close as he reloaded his rifle.

Thomas reloaded his own weapon, snapping it back against his chest just as the sounds of gunfire and shouting began to die down. He looked around and saw the other soldiers standing still, their rifles ready, waiting in tense silence for the next command. Thomas listened but could only hear Kelly sobbing softly over Jack's body.

Quietly, Thomas crouched and made his way over to Kelly. He saw Jack's limp body lying across Kelly's legs, his eyes wide open and staring blankly. Kelly's sobs grew harder as he stammered incoherently.

Thomas placed his hand on Kelly's shoulder.

"I'm sorry..."

"Don't!" Kelly snapped, knocking Thomas's hand off his shoulder. "Don't say it. You didn't know him, so don't even try to feel sorry for him."

They finally arrived at base camp in Monroe, North Carolina. The men were each assigned to a bunkhouse, where they would rest when they weren't fighting on the front lines. Thomas, Billy, and Jo were bunked together, along with Kelly and another man named Marvin.

The men weren't given any time to settle in before being ordered to the front. From then on, time became meaningless. The time spent on the battlefield had already felt like a lifetime, while the time spent at camp was fleeting—barely enough to sit for a moment before being sent back to the chaos of war.

Before any of the men knew it, it was already July. They'd been at the front for two months, witnessing things they wished they could unsee. They'd only spent two days resting at base camp before being sent back to the field, where they stayed for a week or longer at a time.

Thomas could barely pull the trigger; his hands were sweaty and weak. He was ducked down behind sandbags stacked only four high, with no room to move between the men crouched beside him. Billy was hunched over next to Thomas, ready to shoot. They had been out in the blistering heat for six days without sleep, surviving on a few pieces of jerky and half-empty canteens.

Thomas glanced at Billy and saw that he, too, was drained of energy. His lips were cracked and bleeding, his eyes were bloodshot and half-closed, and he was shooting at nothing.

Thomas yanked Billy's arm.

"Come on, Billy, let's get back to camp!" he shouted over the rapid gunfire.

Billy shook his head and stood up, only for Thomas to pull him right back down.

"Are you nuts?" Thomas yelled. "Come on! We've got to stay low. You want to get shot?"

He grabbed Billy's collar and dragged his near-lifeless companion across the ground.

They finally reached the forest behind the battlefield, where they stopped to rest. The forest was half the size of what it used to be when the war had first begun. The constant gunfire and cannon blasts had wiped out nearly all the trees. Fortunately, their base camp wasn't dependent on the forest for cover.

Billy stood up, gazing out at the battlefield. He couldn't even see half a mile through the thick smoke.

"What did we get ourselves into, Thomas?"

"I don't know," Thomas answered blankly.

Billy shot a glance at him. "Did you hear that?"

"What?"

"There! Someone's calling for help."

Before Thomas could respond, Billy started running toward the sound.

"No! Billy, where are—?"

Thomas tried grabbing him, but he was already gone. He desperately ran after Billy, determined to bring him back to safety. Finally, he caught up to him and whipped him around.

"Are you crazy?" Thomas yelled. "Are you trying to get yourself killed?"

"Don't you hear him?" Billy insisted.

"Billy, you're exhausted. You're just imagining—"

Thomas stopped mid-sentence.

"Help! Someone, anyone, help!" a voice yelled out.

"Now you hear him, don't you?" Billy said, chasing after the sound.

As they came closer, the cries became clearer and more recognizable. They finally reached the source and realized that it was Kelly.

"Finally! I thought no one would hear me," Kelly said breathlessly. "We have to help this man back to camp. He's bleeding badly. Please, help me—he's too heavy to carry on my own."

Thomas grabbed one of the unconscious man's arms. His face was unrecognizable, covered in dirt, mud, and ash. Kelly grabbed the other arm and Billy led the way, the thick smoke shielding them from enemy fire. Kelly and Thomas watched the tree line of the forest until it disappeared in a flash that blinded them and threw them to the ground.

Thomas rolled onto his back and found himself unable to move. His entire body felt numb. He tried to sit up, but all he could do was lie there and look around. He saw Billy and tried to call out to him, but no sound came from his mouth.

With all the strength he had left, Thomas focused on Billy, who was crouched over him. Billy's lips moved, but Thomas couldn't hear what he was saying. In fact, Thomas couldn't even hear the gunfire anymore—just a buzzing noise that turned into a sharp ringing.

Thomas tried to concentrate on Billy, but his vision blurred. Everything went dark and silent. The last thing Thomas saw was Ily.

12

ILY

Three months had passed since Carol's funeral and Carl's birth. Ily had been helping Betsy and her family with chores and errands. Betsy had been experiencing a whirlwind of emotions: she felt incredibly blessed to have her new son, but devastated by the loss of her baby girl. Ily tried her best to avoid adding any stress to Betsy—or to herself.

Lately, Ily hadn't been feeling well either. Her stomach had been twisting and turning, and she couldn't shake the feeling that something was terribly wrong. She decided that she would mention it to Dr. Rogers during her five-month check-up. On her way out to see him, Eddie stopped her and asked if she could pick up more cloth for diapers.

Dr. Rogers gave Ily a weak smile as she stepped through the door. He looked irritated and tense.

"I'll be right with you, Ily. Just have a seat," he said before disappearing behind the curtains.

Ily sat down and noticed the front page of the newspaper on the table. The bold headline mentioned more about the Dust Bowl. She picked it up and began reading the article.

Her eyes widened as she read about dust storms occurring across the states, mostly in the Central and Midwest regions. She gasped as she read that there had been 38 dust storms reported two years ago in

1933, caused by livestock overgrazing, poor farming practices, over-farming, and droughts. The article warned that this year was projected to be the hottest yet, urging everyone to prepare for a potentially non-existent winter.

Winter? That's not for another three or four months, Ily thought. *It's only August. How are we going to survive?*

She was finishing the article when she heard voices behind the curtain.

"You can't have it; I need it," Dr. Rogers was saying.

Then she heard a woman's voice respond, one she instantly recognized: Alice.

"And why not?"

"Alice, you know why."

"I don't care! I want it, and whatever I want, I get."

"Well, not this time!"

"How dare you!" Alice screamed.

"Lower your voice. Mrs. Milton is in my waiting room," Dr. Rogers said firmly.

Ily stared blankly at the curtains, unsure of what to do. She started to stand when Alice burst through the curtains and stormed toward the door, not even acknowledging Ily's presence.

Alice stopped in the doorway and turned around.

"I'll be back for my automobile, Almanzo, and this time I'll have my daddy with me!" she yelled before running out in tears.

Ily let out a deep breath and stood up. Dr. Rogers emerged from behind the curtain, now smiling. Ily couldn't believe he could smile after what had just happened, but she simply smiled back politely.

"Sorry about that," Dr. Rogers said, pointing toward the door. "How are you doing on this fine day?"

Ily cleared her throat. "Fine, I guess. Well, I'm not sure."

"Then step into my office, and we'll talk," he said warmly.

Ily walked into the office and immediately caught the lingering scent of Alice's lavender-and-vanilla perfume. The smell comforted her; it reminded her of her grandmother, who had used the same scent to help Ily sleep as a child. Even now, Ily would sometimes spray it when she felt alone—especially with Thomas away.

Dr. Rogers interrupted her thoughts as he gently helped her onto the examination table. The table stood on the left side of the small room, while a wardrobe and a bucket of water sat on a counter with a cupboard above it on the opposite wall.

"There you are. Are you comfortable? What seems to be the problem?"

Ily was silent at first, rubbing her belly. "All last week, I've been getting this strange feeling that something is wrong, but I can't figure it out. The more I try to think about it, the sicker I feel. Sometimes I almost vomit. I just want to make sure our child is okay."

Dr. Rogers unwrapped his stethoscope and placed the earbuds in his ears. He then glided the diaphragm over her chest and stomach, moving it slowly in a circular motion.

"Have you felt any pain in your chest or stomach?"

"No, it's nothing like that. I just have this sick feeling. I don't know how to explain it."

Dr. Rogers smiled as he continued listening.

"What is it?" Ily asked, noticing his expression.

"Here," he said, removing the earbuds and placing them gently in Ily's ears. "Do you hear anything?"

Ily listened and smiled.

"Is that…?"

"Yes, that's the heartbeat—loud and clear, as perfect as it can be."

Ily sighed in relief, tears forming in her eyes.

"Oh, if only Thomas were here to hear this," she said softly.

"How is Thomas doing?" Dr. Rogers asked.

Ily sniffed and cleared her throat. "He's doing well, as far as I know. In his last letter, he said he was on his way to the front. They were almost there when they got ambushed!"

Ily noticed the worried look on Dr. Rogers' face and quickly reassured him.

"Oh, he's alright! They took cover in time. But before they did, Thomas said one of the men was shot. I sent him a letter to make sure he's okay, but I haven't gotten a reply yet." She frowned deeply.

"Ily, are you alright?" Dr. Rogers asked.

"There's that feeling again."

"What does it feel like?"

"Like a knot tightening."

Dr. Rogers listened to her stomach again, his expression serious.

"Well, the baby's okay."

"It's a bad feeling, like something is going awfully wrong—or already has," Ily said as a tear rolled down her cheek.

"Maybe you're still grieving Carol's death, and with Carl's birth, everyone's emotions are mixed up right now. It'll pass shortly, I promise," Dr. Rogers said with a warm smile.

"It feels like more than that, though."

"Do you think it's..." He paused.

"Thomas?" Ily said it for him as another tear escaped her eye.

Dr. Rogers gently wiped it away.

"I'm sure he's fine. You just told me he sent you a letter. You can't worry about what you can't see or change, especially in your condition. Your baby needs your strength to keep growing. Tell you what: the next time you get this feeling, write it down on a piece of paper."

He left the room briefly and returned with a notepad and pencil.

"Here. Any thoughts—good or bad—jot them down. Give your worries to the paper. Okay?"

Ily stared at the pad.

"It works, trust me," Dr. Rogers said. "I do this every time Alice comes and goes. I write all my thoughts about her, and then I feel a lot better."

He held the pad out to her again with a grin.

Ily took the paper and smiled back at him.

"I'll try it."

Ily crossed the street to the mercantile, a small store owned by an older couple, Hank and Hattie Ness. They had taken over the store after the death of Hattie's uncle, inheriting both the store and the small cottage behind it. Hank and Hattie had given their house to one of their five children to support their family of six. Their other children also lived in Keyes with their families.

Hank and Hattie, who'd emigrated from Ireland just after their wedding fifty years ago, had five children: Anthony, Susan, Robert, Walter, and Rose. Over the years, their children had blessed them with a total of twenty-three grandchildren. Although Hank and Hattie's children had been saddened by the passing of Hattie's uncle, they were happy to see their parents take over the mercantile, knowing it would keep them busy and happy.

Hattie was organizing some new deliveries when Ily stepped through the front doors of the mercantile.

"Mornin', Ily," Hattie said in her strong Irish accent.

"Good morning, Mrs. Ness. How are you?"

"Oh, just gran'. And you?"

"Alright, I guess."

"You feeling gran', m'dear?" Hattie asked as Ily sighed.

"No, not really. I've just been having some strange feelings in my stomach."

Hattie's eyes widened. "It's not your baby, is it?"

"Oh no. In fact, I just came from Dr. Rogers' office, and he says the baby is just fine. Very healthy, in fact. Strong heartbeat and all."

Hattie relaxed. "That is very gran' news. So, then, what's the matter?"

"He thinks it's stress."

"Why is that?" Hattie asked.

"Well, I've been thinking about Thomas a lot lately, and every time I do, I get this tight knot in the pit of my stomach. And I get lonely," Ily said, her voice trembling.

"Well, that's normal, dear. You just miss him, that's all."

"But it feels like more than that. I just have this sense that tomorrow I'm going to get a letter about him, not from him."

A tear raced down Ily's cheek. Hattie wrapped her arms around her and embraced her tightly.

"When was the last time you heard from him, m'dear?"

Ily thought for a moment, and her eyes widened. She hadn't even considered it when she told Dr. Rogers about the ambush: that was the last letter she'd received from Thomas, back in May. Ily burst into tears, realizing something was wrong. Thomas never forgot to write; he always sent a letter every other week.

"Oh, goodness. Whatever is it?" Hattie said concernedly.

"May!" Ily blurted out in between sobs.

"May?"

Ily nodded and tried to explain, but she could only continue to bawl incoherently.

"Ah, honey, you're goin' to have to slow down and catch your breath, for I can't understand one word."

Ily collected herself, apologized, and started over.

"I remember his last letter. It was back in May. He used to send one every other week, but I haven't gotten one since then."

Ily gasped and grabbed her stomach. "There's that feeling again. Oh, I just know something is wrong."

"Now, you best stop that, or you will have somethin' wrong," Hattie said. "You mustn't worry. You just have to trust that the Lord will keep Thomas out of harm's way—keep them all out of harm's way. And, Ily, if you ever need to talk, you can stop by anytime, even late at night. I'll be here for you. Even Hank will listen."

They both burst out into giggles.

"Uh-oh! I heard m'name, followed by laughter. That can't be a good sign," Hank chuckled as he walked in. "Well, hello, Ily. And how you be on this fine day?"

"Oh, doing a little better now, with Hattie here," Ily replied with a smile.

"Well, that's what Hattie does best—turns a gray day into a gran' one, with just a twinkle in her eye."

"Oh, Hank." Hattie gave him a playful shove, and they all laughed again.

Mr. Ness helped Ily gather supplies for the Ryesons and herself. She thanked them again before walking out the door.

After giving Eddie and Betsy their groceries, Ily headed home. As she reached the top of the hill near the old shack, she noticed Thomas's field and was overwhelmed with shock: all his crops had been destroyed by the dust storms. She couldn't believe that dust could ruin entire fields of crops. She remembered hearing men in town talk about how the storms had not only wiped out their crops but claimed their livestock, as dust, dirt, and mud clogged the animals' lungs and stomachs. Ily shook her head at the thought. She looked up toward the sky and prayed for rain.

The next morning, Ily rose early to finish setting up the nursery for her baby, who Dr. Rogers had told her would be due sometime in December—just four months away. Ily's belly wasn't huge yet, but it was starting to show.

Around ten o'clock, Ily stepped out onto her porch and was shaking out her dusty rag when she spotted Mr. Kay walking past her house. She glanced at her empty mailbox and felt a pang of confusion and anxiety. She called out to Mr. Kay and ran out to meet him.

"Still no mail?"

"I'm sorry, Mrs. Milton. Just the bills I gave you yesterday."

Mr. Kay noticed the concern in her eyes and tried to ease her mind.

"He'll write, I just know it. He always does, right? I'm sure right now he's sitting with a pen and paper, deciding what to write. With so much happening, he probably doesn't want to scare you."

Mr. Kay wiped a tear from Ily's eye. Ily nodded silently and headed back to the nursery.

As the sun began to set, Ily realized that her work was almost complete. She didn't know what she would do once the nursery was all set up. Cleaning and organizing seemed to be all she could do to keep her mind off of Thomas.

13

THOMAS

Thomas woke to the sound of a cannon jolting him out of his cot. "What was that?"

He looked over to Billy and Jo's cot, but neither of them was there. He glanced toward the tent flaps and saw that it was still nighttime.

Where'd they go? he wondered. *It's got to be two, three in the morning.*

He walked over to the tent flaps and tried to peek outside, but it was pitch black. He was about to give up and go back to bed when he heard a woman scream. He froze, confused; there were no women in this army.

The scream came again, sharper this time. Shaking off his hesitation, Thomas stepped outside. As soon as he did, a blinding white light forced him to shield his eyes. Slowly, the light dimmed, narrowing to a single bulb which hung over a bed. A woman lay on it, sweat plastering her hair to her face and obscuring her features. She was panting heavily, trying to catch her breath.

Thomas stepped closer and noticed several people standing around the bed, smiling down at the woman. He looked closer and was shocked to see familiar faces: Eddie, Betsy, Billy, and Jo.

"Eddie? Betsy? What are you guys doing here?" Thomas called out, but no one responded. He shouted again, louder this time, but still, nothing.

Thomas approached the foot of the bed, straining to see the woman's face. Just as he reached out to brush her hair aside, Betsy grabbed him, pulling him into a hug. Thomas saw her lips moving, but he couldn't hear a word she was saying.

Then Eddie and Billy stepped forward, brushing the hair away from the woman's face. Thomas's eyes widened in recognition.

"Ily?" he whispered.

She looked up at him, her face breaking into a smile.

"It's time," she said.

"Time?" Thomas repeated.

Just then, Ily lifted a small bundle wrapped in a blanket. Cradling the baby, she held it up for Thomas to see. Her smile grew brighter.

"It's a..."

Thomas's eyes fluttered open. At first, he saw only blinding whiteness. Slowly, his surroundings came into focus: white walls, white floors, and white cots. Turning his head, he noticed a man sleeping in the cot beside him. Then another man stepped into view—an older man with wild, curly white hair, dressed in a white uniform. The man's mouth was moving, but the words sounded distant and unclear. Thomas blinked, trying to focus. When he opened his eyes again, the old man's face was much closer.

"...feelin'?" Thomas heard as the man came into view.

Thomas didn't respond.

"Yer one lucky son of a gun! Fry mah hide! You know that?" the old man continued in a thick backwoods accent.

"Wh-what?" Thomas croaked, his body feeling weak and sore. Even speaking was painful.

"Yup. You an' yer friends. That mine coulda killed y'all!"

Thomas sat up abruptly.

"WHAT?" he shouted, his heart racing.

"Woah, now!" the man said. "You need t'settle down, as any fool kin plainly see. Do you know yer name and where yer at? Can you remember anything?"

Thomas ignored the question, catching only one word. "Friends?"

"Yes, sir—friends. That's what I said. Private Kelly and the other young man without dog tags. Unless you don't have friends, but I don't knows you!" the man chuckled. "Now, do you know yer name?"

"Billy?" Thomas asked, his voice trembling, anxious to know the whereabouts of his young companion.

"Huh?" The old man gave him a confused look, then glanced down at the dog tags in his hand. "That's not yer name. I knows 'cause I'm lookin' at yer tags. Do you know yer name?"

"Of course. It's Thomas. I'm stationed at Monroe, North Carolina. But I'm not sure where I am now," Thomas replied, glancing around the unfamiliar room.

"There we go. Mighty fine. I can answer yer question. Right now, you're at Medical Camp 430. It's jus' outside of Base Camp—a hop, skip, an' a jump away. Though, in yer condition, you shouldn't be hoppin', skippin', or jumpin'! Jus' try t'lay still."

The man chuckled again, then cleared his throat at the sight of Thomas's unamused expression.

"Mah name's Doctor William Whittle. But you can jus' call me Doc Whittle. Oh, and about Billy Joe—he's fine. The mine didn't even touch him. In fact, he and another man pulled y'all outta there jus' in the nick of time. One of you stepped on a mine and went flyin'. Luckily, it was a dud. We still had t'pull some shrapnel outta ya, but it coulda been a lot worse—at least, for you and Kelly. Now, I can't say the same for the man without the dog tags. He was already wounded bad before the mine—lost a lotta blood, cuss in all tarnation. But thanks to Billy Joe, y'all made it here in time. Otherwise, that soldier woulda died out there."

Dr. Whittle's voice faded into the background as Thomas tried to process what he'd just heard.

"Actually, it was Kelly who found the soldier and yelled for help," Thomas recalled. "Billy and I heard him and went to see what was going on. I helped Kelly, and that's when everything went black."

"Well, it's mighty fine t'see you still have yer memory. Now, you git some rest, ya hear? You've been out for four whole weeks."

"What?" Thomas exclaimed.

"Yeah, I knows. Tell me about it. I thunk for sure you weren't gonna wake up for a whole 'nother month. But I was surely wrong about that, thank the heavens!"

"Thomas?"

Thomas turned to see Billy standing in the doorway. Billy rushed down the center aisle, which was lined with at least a dozen cots on either side. Thomas noticed that only a few other cots were occupied by wounded soldiers.

Billy hugged him tightly, making Thomas grunt in pain.

"Oh, Tom! Sorry, you alright?" Billy asked, stepping back.

"Yeah, just a little sore," Thomas replied.

"Oh, yeah, he's jus' fine there, Billy Joe!" Dr. Whittle interjected.

"Uh, just Billy," Billy said awkwardly.

"Don't worry, Billy Joe—jus' a couple bruised ribs and a few bumps and cuts, but nothin' too serious," Dr. Whittle said, glancing back and forth between Thomas and Billy with a quirky smile.

"I can't say that about t'other two, though. Well, with Kelly, I can, but with No-Dog-Tag Man? I'm not countin' on him t'wake up too soon. You know he was in surgery for almost a day? Yeah, isn't that somethin'?" Well, of course you didn't know, Thomas—you were in a coma too. But isn't that interestin'? They say he had twelve bullets in him, cuss in all tarnation. They did a purdy good job on his right leg, too! If they hadn't done what they did, he'd have lost it. Yup, I'm sure proud of my surgeons."

He flashed another zany smile.

"Well, I got other patients t'look in on, so I'll leave you two t'chat."

Turning to Billy, he added, "Now, only stay for a few minutes. Thomas needs his rest to recover. He needs t'gain his strength back. Just 'cause he's been out for a month doesn't mean he's been sleepin'. He still needs plenty of rest."

Thomas and Billy watched as Dr. Whittle exited through the doors that Billy had come through.

"Jeez, I thought he'd never leave," Billy muttered.

"I thought he'd never stop talking," Thomas added.

Thomas was released from the infirmary the following week. Dr. Whittle told him that he had recovered nicely, and expressed hope that Kelly and the man with no tags would also wake up soon. As Thomas was preparing to leave, Dr. Whittle reminded him to stay off the minefields and laughed so hard his eyes began to tear. Thomas smiled and rolled his eyes as he walked away.

For the next few days, Thomas tried to lay low and rest up, as he still hadn't been cleared to return to the front, which was fine with him. He spent much of his time visiting Kelly and the other man, sitting between their beds on the floor and talking to them. He talked about what was happening in the war, how his day was going, whether he was feeling any pain, and all about Ily back home. He even told them that he was going to be a father.

Just then, a thought crossed his mind: Ily would be alone when the baby was born. Sure, she would have Betsy and Eddie, but they had their own children to worry about. The baby would be fatherless until the war was over—and what if the war never ended? He felt a wave of sadness come over him, knowing he would miss the birth of his first child.

Then a crazy idea—crazier than the war itself—took shape in his mind. He stood up and began searching for Billy. He first looked in the mess hall, but Billy wasn't there. Then he checked the rec tent, but still no sign of him. Finally, he found Billy sitting on his cot in their tent, reading letters from home.

"Billy!" Thomas called out.

"Thomas! Hey, how you feelin'?" Billy asked, looking up from his letters. "You wanna know something? My sister Sarah is about to turn ten. Can you believe that? Double digits! She's so excited—her birthday's next month, and then Jason's gonna be eight in December. Golly, I could be there—uh, I mean, I wish I could be there."

Thomas ignored his own confusion, his mind occupied with something much more pressing.

"Well, why can't you be there?" he asked Billy.

Billy looked puzzled. "What are you talking about? You know why I can't be there. I made a choice to be here. I have a duty to fulfill."

"I'm saying, what if we run away?"

Billy's jaw dropped. "WHAT? What do you mean, run away?"

Thomas shushed him. "Lower your voice! I'm serious."

"Thomas, tell me you're joking. You aren't thinking straight. That mine hit you harder than the doctor thought. You've got splinters in your mind wheel. I mean, what if we get caught? You've seen what they do to deserters. They either get caught by the other side and become prisoners—or worse. And if you're lucky and get caught by our side, well, they won't kill you, but they'll do something to make sure you stay."

"But do you know why those guys get caught?" Thomas countered.

"Why?"

"They don't have a plan. They just run without thinking. Wait—what do you mean, you made a choice?"

"What?" Billy stammered, suddenly nervous. "You were telling me why they get caught," he said, trying to change the subject.

"I didn't have a choice. Eddie didn't have a choice. None of the men who went through boot camp had a choice. What are you talking about?" Thomas pressed. Billy looked guilty. "Billy, what aren't you telling me?"

Billy took a deep breath. "Alright. I'm not really eighteen."

"What? How old are you?" Thomas asked, shocked.

"Fifteen," Billy admitted nervously.

"Fifteen? Billy, you're just a child!"

"I am not!" Billy argued back.

"Wait," Thomas said, thinking for a moment. "Didn't your father die when you were fourteen?"

"Yes. That's why I'm here—for my family. After he died, I turned fifteen and became the man of the house. I realized my family wasn't doing well, so I thought if I ran away and became a soldier, I could send my earnings home to help my ma with the farm and my younger siblings. I did it for them. Please don't tell anyone—I'd get kicked out."

"Of course you would—you're just a child."

"Stop calling me that!" Billy snapped.

"Alright, you're not a child," Thomas conceded. "But still, you're way too young to be here. Now, more than ever, I know we should run away."

They sat in silence until Billy finally spoke.

"So, do you have a plan?"

"Well, no."

Billy rolled his eyes.

"But we will," Thomas assured him. "It only took us, what, half a week to get here? Including stops? So, if we start planning now, we could leave in a couple of months. That way, we'll work out all the kinks—you'll make it home just in time for Jason's birthday, and I'll make it home just in time to become a father."

"In a couple of months? It might be snowy!"

"That's why we start planning now. We can prepare for whatever comes our way—snow, enemies, or anything else. Plus, it'll give us plenty of time to factor in the weather and make sure we get home. But this has to stay just between us. Alright?"

"Of course. Wait—what about Jo?"

"No," Thomas said firmly. "It might look suspicious if three men leave at the same time. Two is already risky." His tone softened as Billy nodded. "Now, if we could just get hold of a map to show—"

Thomas was cut off when Dr. Whittle burst into their bunk.

"Thomas! Billy Joe! Great—you're both here."

They exchanged puzzled glances before looking back at Dr. Whittle.

"Come quickly—it's Kelly!"

"Is he alright?" Thomas asked, concerned.

"What?" Dr. Whittle paused, catching his breath. "Oh, yes, sir—he's fine! Fry mah hide, he jus' woke up, that's all."

And with that, he dashed back out.

"He's kind of strange, isn't he?" Billy remarked.

Thomas nodded.

They found Dr. Whittle by Kelly's bed, talking to him animatedly.

"You're one lucky son of a gun? You know that? You and your friends, that is! That mine could've killed all three of you!" he exclaimed, repeating what he'd told Thomas. As Thomas and Billy entered, Dr. Whittle waved them over.

"Now, he jus' woke up. I figured you two'd want to see him." He motioned for them to approach Kelly's bed. "Don't stay too long—he needs his rest. Jus' because he was in a coma for six weeks doesn't mean he got any sleep, alright?"

He chuckled and moved on to his next patient.

"Thomas? What happened?" Kelly asked weakly.

Thomas stood next to Kelly's white cot. "Do you remember anything?"

"I remember seeing a man down. I tried to lift him, but he was stuck or something. I couldn't move him. So I called out for help. It was too dark; I couldn't see anything. I was afraid no one could hear me until I saw you, I think."

Kelly paused, trying to recall.

"That's all I can remember. I don't know if that man is okay or if it was you—or how I even got here. How *did* I get here? And where *is* here?"

He looked around, taking in the stark white walls. For a moment, he thought he might be in heaven.

"That's all true," Thomas reassured him. "But you don't remember anything else?"

"No, I don't! I would tell you if I did," Kelly replied, his voice rising.

"Alright, I'm just trying to help," Thomas said, raising his hands innocently.

"Well, does he look familiar?" Billy asked, stepping aside so Kelly could see the man in the cot next to him.

"That him?"

"Yeah. You and I were carrying him when we stepped on a mine," Thomas explained. "Luckily, it was defective—just strong enough to knock us into comas but not kill us."

"You were in a coma, too?" Kelly asked, surprised.

"He sure was—for a whole month. He nearly scared me to death," Billy answered.

"Alright, that explains that. But how did we get here? Billy couldn't have carried all of us!"

"No. Other men heard the explosion and ran over. They carried us here," Thomas said.

Suddenly they heard someone groan in pain. Their heads turned toward the man in the cot.

"Dr. Whittle? Dr. Whittle?" Thomas called, looking around but not seeing him.

"Of course—when you don't want him, he's everywhere, but when you do, he's nowhere to be found," he muttered as he ran out the door to find him.

Billy knelt next to the cot and patted the man's shoulder. "It's alright, sir. Help is on the way."

The man gasped. "Help, help—I need help!" He coughed weakly. "Please, I've been shot."

"Sir, you're alright now. You're in a medical camp. The doctor is almost here," Billy reassured him, glancing at the door just as it flew open.

"Alright, alright, outta my way! The doc is in the house! I've always wanted t'say that!" Dr. Whittle announced as he bustled in.

"Who is this guy?" Kelly asked, staring at Dr. Whittle bewilderedly.

Thomas rolled his eyes as Dr. Whittle turned to face Kelly.

"Doc Whittle's the name, and patchin' patients up is mah game!" he squawked. "Now, let's take a look, shall we?" he said, turning toward the injured man.

"Are you the only doctor?" Kelly asked skeptically.

"Well, of course not. Duh. Jus' the only one right now! Alright, now what seems t'be the problem?"

"Please," the injured man coughed again.

Dr. Whittle squatted next to him. "How do you feel?"

The man's breathing was labored. "I need help. I've been shot. Please, I need a doctor. Help." His voice was weak.

"It's okay. You're at a medical camp. You've been through surgery, and we gotcha all patched up. You're gonna be okay. How d'ya feel? Do you remember anything?" Dr. Whittle asked, waiting as the man stared blankly.

"Please...help." The man's tone grew angrier.

Dr. Whittle glanced back at the others. "I reckon he's jus' in shock."

He turned back to the man.

"Sir, yer alright now. Us doctors took mighty fine care of you. You don't need help no more. Now I need you to help me in figuring out yer name. Can you tell me what yer name is?"

He waited for a response. "Please, sir, can you tell me your name?"

"Droo..." the man whispered faintly.

"What in tarnation? Can ya speak up?"

"Please, doctor, I need help. I've—"

"Yes, sir, I knows, and we helped you. Now, can you help me with yer name?"

"Is he alright, Doctor?" Kelly asked.

Dr. Whittle turned around. "Yes—um, he's jus' in shock. He should snap out of it soon. It's common in these types of patients. We jus' need t'take it slow and keep calm, dawgone it."

Thomas was taken aback by Dr. Whittle's sudden change in attitude.

"Sir, I need yer name. Can you tell me yer name?"

The man didn't respond.

"Alright, let's try somethin'," Dr. Whittle said. "Sir, can you hear me? Blink if you can hear me," he whispered.

He waited, staring into the man's eyes.

The man just stared at the ceiling, then slowly shut his eyes and opened them again. Dr. Whittle smiled, and the others sighed with relief. The man blinked again and again.

"Fry mah hide! Now we're gittin' somewhere. Alright, sir, I'm gonna check your vitals now, okay?"

The man blinked again as Dr. Whittle put his stethoscope buds into his ears and listened to his heart and blood pressure. He nodded as he listened, then checked the man's pupils for dilation.

"Well, your blood pressure and temp are normal, I reckon. Alright, now let's see if you can wiggle your fingers and toes."

He pulled the sheet down and watched the man attempt to move.

The man was dressed in a long white hospital gown that hung loosely on his frail frame. Thomas could see his ribs poking out through the fabric. His legs were as thin as toothpicks, and his feet were rough and cracked, with dried blood where blisters had been. Scarlet-stained bandages were wrapped around his right leg.

They all watched as Dr. Whittle ran a finger along the bottom of the man's foot. The man jerked his foot in response.

"Great! Now, can you move your fingers?"

It took the man some effort, but he slowly raised his arms and wiggled his fingers.

"Good, excellent! This means you're not paralyzed!" Dr. Whittle grinned.

"Droo…" the man whispered again.

Dr. Whittle leaned closer. "What?"

"Drew. My name is Drew," the man said more clearly.

Dr. Whittle's grin widened. "Well, Drew, it's mighty nice t'make your acquaintance." He shook Drew's hand. "Do you remember anything? Or why yer here?"

They all watched as Drew wrestled with his memory.

"It's okay. Why don't you get some rest? It might come back to ya. Okay?"

Drew nodded weakly and closed his eyes.

"Uh, Drew?" Dr. Whittle called out.

Drew's eyes snapped back open.

"Okay, jus' checkin'! G'night!"

Dr. Whittle turned toward the others and beamed.

"We've made a lot of progress today! First Thomas, then Kelly, and now look—we even know No-Dog-Tag Man's name!" He gestured towards their new companion. "Drew!"

He then turned to Kelly. "Now, Kelly, you're as fine as pickle juice, but you need t'rest jus' the same. Jus' because you were in a coma—"

"Yeah, yeah, yeah, we know; it doesn't mean we got any sleep," Thomas interrupted, finishing the doctor's sentence.

Dr. Whittle looked at him in surprise. "Have I said that before?"

Thomas and Billy rolled their eyes.

A week later, Thomas and Billy went to check on Kelly and Drew. As they walked in, they noticed that Kelly's bed was empty, and Drew was sitting up in his bed, writing. Drew spotted them and quickly stuffed his papers under his mattress.

"Where's Kelly?" Thomas asked.

Drew glanced toward Kelly's bed. "Latrine. He went to the latrine."

"What were you writing?" Billy asked.

"That? Oh, nothing—just a letter to my mother. You know how mothers get if they don't know where you are at all times." Drew laughed nervously.

"Yeah, don't I ever. Mothers!" Billy scoffed.

Thomas cleared his throat. "So, how are you feeling? Any better? Have you remembered anything?"

"It's starting to come back—slowly. Not much, though." But I do remember…I was trying to head for cover, then the next thing I knew…. someone noticed me and shot me. But I killed him before he could kill me.

Drew looked up from his thoughts. "Sorry, I think I just remembered something."

"What is it?" Thomas asked.

"I don't know; it's fuzzy. Anyway, after I got hit, I started crawling to the woods but couldn't make it. If your friend—uh, Kelly?"

Thomas nodded.

"If it wasn't for him tripping over me," Drew continued, "I'd have died out there. When he found me, I wasn't in good enough shape to walk, so he tried to carry me. Then…I don't know what happened after that. I figure something bad happened, seeing as my rescuer is lying in the bed next to mine."

"Don't blame me! It wasn't my fault," Kelly argued as he walked in. "It was the dumb South Carolinians. They're the ones who put that stupid mine there." He scoffed. "How the heck did they even get on our side to dig it, anyway?"

"What? What do you mean, we stepped on that mine?" Drew asked, his voice filled with concern.

Kelly was about to respond when he realized what Drew had said. "What do you mean by '*that* mine'? Do you know something we don't?"

Drew started to sweat but feigned ignorance. "What?"

"You said, 'What do you mean, we hit that mine?'"

"Oh…I said that?" Drew replied, trying to sound casual.

All three of them slowly nodded their heads. Drew stared at them tensely for a moment and exhaled.

"Alright, you caught me. I was the one who dug that mine."

"What?" Kelly exclaimed.

Drew raised his hands defensively. "Not for you guys—or North Carolina—but for the South! In case any of them ever tried to cross over to this side to get better aim or something," he explained, somewhat unconvincingly.

"Oh, that makes sense…I guess," Kelly said, clearly not sold on Drew's story.

"Well, it sounds like yer memory is back!" Dr. Whittle cheered.

Thomas and Billy turned and saw Dr. Whittle standing right behind them.

"When did you get here?" Billy blurted.

"Oh, yeah…" Drew said slowly. "I guess I remember a lot more than I thought."

In fact, he remembered everything from before the blast. *I'm Drew Melvin*, he thought to himself. *I know my age: 36. I know my birthday: June ninth, 1899. I know that I'm from Georgia. I know exactly who I am, where I'm supposed to be, who I'm fighting for, and who sent me here. I also know I have a duty to fulfill, and I can't do it with all these ninnies here. These foolish men tried to kill me with my own mine.*

"That's good, right?" Drew asked aloud. "That means I can be cleared and sent out of here?"

"It's better than good—it's excellent!" said Dr. Whittle. "I don't see why today can't be the day. You've had plenty of rest to get yer strength back. I'll jus' have to check you out, and then you can be on yer way with yer friends—including you, Mr. Kelly!"

"Just Kelly," Kelly said.

"Oh, sorry, Mr. Kelly," Dr. Whittle said with a grin before walking away.

"It'll be good to get out, won't it, Kelly?" Drew asked as he got dressed.

"Not really. Look what's out there: war," Kelly answered grimly.

"Alrighty-ho, here we go!" Dr. Whittle said, returning with the release forms. "Now, I jus' need your signatures, and you can be on yer way."

He handed Drew his form and then gave Kelly his.

"I see why you hoof it out with Mr. Kelly," he said as the men signed the forms. "Mr. *Eunice* Kelly, that is", he added with a smirk, scurrying out of the room. Moments later, loud laughter could be heard from behind the closed doors.

Kelly's face turned scarlet. He signed his name, threw the papers onto the bed, and stormed out the door.

Thomas and Billy led Drew out and showed him around the camp. Thomas told Drew he could bunk with them since they happened to have an empty cot in their bunkhouse. Next, they took Drew to the mess hall to get him some food. As they walked through the army tent doors, they were hit by the smell of two-day-old food and burnt coffee. Drew just about gagged at the odor, while Thomas couldn't help but smile.

"You'll get used to it," he assured Drew.

Drew glanced around and noticed that the walls were made of weather-worn canvas, covered with patched-up holes. The windows were plastic and let in very little light. Looking up, he saw only seven light bulbs illuminating the tent. As they continued walking, he counted ten tables on each side of the middle aisle, which led them to the beginning of the food line.

Each of them grabbed a metal tray and stood in line behind a few other men. Three cooks served food as they slid their trays down the counter. One slopped on some type of meat with gravy, the next added mixed vegetables, and the last gave them a hard piece of bread along with a cup of burnt coffee.

As they walked away from the line, Drew lifted his tray to his nose but pulled it away as the stench hit him.

"Ugh! Does it always smell this bad?"

"It looks and smells worse than it tastes—which is surprising," Billy quipped. Drew gave him a crooked smile.

They found Kelly sitting alone at a table near the door.

"Mind if we join you?" Thomas asked.

Kelly shrugged his shoulders as Drew sat next to him, while Thomas and Billy sat across the table.

Drew took a bite of his food and immediately spat it out.

Kelly cleared his throat, smiling. "It takes a little getting used to."

"Ugh, this food is disgusting!" Drew exclaimed. "It's not even fit for a horse. And I don't even dare to touch the coffee—who knows how long that's been sitting in the pot. Where I come from, we had fresh coffee twice a day with fresh meat; no mystery meat surprise. They fed us like kings."

"Well, of course, food's going to be better back home than here. You think they actually give a crap about us? They just want us to fight and win for them," Kelly scoffed.

Thomas, however, stared at Drew confusedly.

"'They?'" Billy started to ask, but Thomas stopped him.

"Where did you come from?" Thomas asked Drew.

"Just through the…" Drew paused. "Just, uh, over the mountains in a town called Griffin, Georgia."

"Griffin, Georgia? Never heard of it."

"Well, it's a small town."

"All the way from Georgia, and you're fighting for North Carolina?"

"Yeah, why?" Drew's tone grew suspicious.

"Oh, nothing. I just assumed that since you live in Georgia, you'd be fighting for South Carolina," Thomas said.

"Yeah, well, I did get summoned for South Carolina."

"Really?"

"Yes, but then North Carolina sent me a summons, and they, uh, had a better deal. So here I am, fighting with you guys."

"Ah, I see. That's interesting."

Drew was annoyed now. "Why is that?" he asked through gritted teeth, his eyes narrowing.

"I was just wondering. Don't get upset; I didn't mean anything by it," Thomas explained, trying to sound apologetic. "I'm just trying to figure out who Drew Melvin is. I'm sorry if I upset you."

"Jeez, Thomas. Not everyone can be a saint like you," Kelly snapped.

"No, it's alright," Drew said. "He has a right—a right to ask and a right to know." He stood up. "I'm going to get some air."

He started to walk away but turned back around and glared at Thomas.

"Just know how far that right can go."

He was gone before Thomas could reply. Kelly stood up and followed Drew out.

Billy turned toward Thomas, looking confused. "What were you trying to get at?"

"I don't know. I was just fishing, I guess. Just trying to get to know him better."

Thomas and Billy left the mess hall and headed back to their bunk to talk more about their escape plan. On the way there, Billy noticed General Hobbs carrying three rolled-up maps.

"Uh, excuse me, General," Billy said with a salute.

"As you were," replied Hobbs in his gravelly voice.

Billy lowered his arm and smiled. "May I ask what you're going to do with those maps?"

"These? They're old, and I'm getting some new ones, so I'm tossing them out."

"Could I have them, sir?"

"What?"

Thomas began to grow nervous and was about to cut in when Billy responded.

"Well, you see, sir, I've never been to school, and my father believed you didn't need any schooling to be a farmer. He never went to school, and my grandfather never did, either. So I've never actually seen what the State looks like."

"State? It's the *United* States. I can see you haven't had any schooling. In that case, here, take them." He handed the maps to Billy. "They're still in pretty good shape—a couple of tears in some spots, but still readable. Young chaps like you should know as much as you can in this cruel world."

"Thank you, sir."

Thomas and Billy saluted again. As they walked away, Thomas gave Billy a look.

"What?" Billy asked defensively. "If we're serious about your plan, then I think we ought to have maps, don't you think?"

They reached the empty tent, unrolled the maps on Thomas's bed, and stared at them.

Billy broke the silence. "What are we thinking, Thomas? Can we really do this?"

Thomas thought more about what they were about to do. He reached for his calendar and pointed to August.

"So it's August, and Ily is due in December. You want to be home before your brother's birthday, which is also in December."

"Thomas, wait. I mean, do you really want to do this? Because if you do, I'm with you all the way. I just want to know why this has come up all of a sudden."

Thomas was quiet.

"Is it Ily? The war? The people? What?" Billy pressed.

"It's Ily *and* the war. When I first got my draft letter, I was all excited to come and help. But now that I'm here, there are things that neither of us will be able to unsee. I've already almost been blown up— and it could have been a lot worse. Ily is going to have a baby. I can't stop thinking about how she could've ended up alone forever. I can't leave her alone. She's battling her own war with the dust storms. Billy, I could've lost her in that storm."

"Okay." Billy nodded in agreement. "Let's do it, then."

He reached for the calendar and thought for a minute.

"What about late November? The weather will be colder, and we'll need to put on more layers and heavy coats. So when we stuff our coats with supplies, people won't be askin' why we look so big. We'll just say we got extra layers on."

"That's a great start, Billy. We also have to think about the pros and cons of this." Thomas looked over the calendar. "Okay, so it's August. If we decide on November, that gives us about"—he ran his finger over the dates as he counted—"eleven weeks to plan and gather supplies. But we also need to remember that it'll probably take us a month to make it home, especially if we're going on foot."

He then grabbed the map and stared at it.

"We're right here," he said, pointing to Monroe, North Carolina. He then pointed between Rockingham and Laurinburg. "Here's where we fight—all along here."

He studied the map further to find Keyes, Oklahoma. He carefully slid his finger across to the middle of the map, trying not to make any of the existing holes bigger. It took a while to find Douglas, Kansas, where Billy lived, and even longer to find his own home, as a hole had begun to form over his hometown. Thomas took a pencil and marked Douglas, Keyes, and the rest of the towns they needed.

"So, November gives us about eleven weeks to plan and gather supplies and any other information. Now, the pros and cons."

Thomas looked up to see Billy studying the route with a confused expression.

"Thomas, how are we going to escape if our route is headed in the same direction as base camp?"

Thomas froze. He hadn't thought of that.

"I think that's a con, isn't it?" Billy added.

Thomas thought for a moment. "I got it! We'll act like we're heading to the front, and when we get deep enough into the woods, we can turn around, sneak past the camp, and head home." He looked at the map again. "Then we'll go through Tennessee to get to Missouri, to Kansas to drop you off, and then I'll head home. We'll need to do some math to see how far it is from state to state, how far from here to your place, and how far from here to mine."

"I can do that!" Billy said. "I love math."

Thomas looked surprised. "Great! If you want to."

"Yeah, my pa taught me all about maps before he died. He used to travel all over delivering hay and crops. I'd always keep track of where he was headed. Math was my best subject in school, too."

"Wait, I thought you'd never been to school."

"Oh, I just told the General that so he'd give me the maps. No, I loved school. After my pa died, I gave up on it. But from time to time, I still practice my math."

Thomas chuckled. "Well, alright then, you're on math duty. That's good, too, 'cause math was my worst subject."

He gave Billy a wink.

"And when you're done," he continued, "we can determine when to leave. We'll have to figure the map out before we can do anything else."

"Thomas, how come you always figure out my lies?" Billy asked suddenly.

Thomas smiled. "Kid, you're a terrible liar—at least, to me, you are."

Billy smiled and shrugged his shoulders. "At least Hobbs didn't figure me out. Well, I better get started."

"I'd hold on. I think someone's comin'. Quick, put everything away."

They finished stuffing their supplies under Thomas's lumpy mattress just as Kelly walked in.

"What are you two doing in here?" Kelly asked.

"Resting before going out on the field again," Billy blurted out.

Kelly rolled his eyes. "You haven't seen Drew, have you?"

"No," Thomas jumped in. "Kelly, since we're alone, maybe we could talk."

"About what?"

"About *who*," Thomas corrected. "Drew."

"Ah, man, now you're talking behind his back? Would you lay off him?"

"Kelly, doesn't he seem suspicious to you?"

"No."

"Really? Why would he bury a mine on the same side he's fighting for?"

"You heard him—in case the South crossed over," Kelly said, his voice beginning to rise.

"He put it all the way behind our men. And doesn't it seem a little odd that he lives in Georgia? The state that supports South Carolina?"

"I don't know, there could be a lot of reasons why. In fact, he told you—the North had better options."

"Do you even know anything about him?" Thomas asked.

"I know enough—just lay off. He's just finished healing, so of course, we don't know much about him yet. And unlike you, I don't need to know everyone's life history. You just like to accuse him of things for no reason."

Kelly stormed out of the tent.

Billy exhaled deeply and turned to Thomas. "That was close. Why do you keep bringing Drew up like he's gone and done somethin' wrong?"

"Because I don't trust him," Thomas said grimly.

"Why?"

"I have this feeling. Ily tells me I have a gift—a sixth sense." Thomas chuckled. "I tell her, no, I just have more common sense than everyone else. But I guess that's how I always figure out your lies, too. Especially the day we saved you—the first day we met. You may have told us you'd slipped, but I could see a different story in your eyes. I see the same thing in Drew's eyes. That's how I can tell when someone's lying."

What do you see?"

"The truth."

"What do you think the truth is?"

"I'm not sure, but I know it's not what he's telling us."

"I don't know, Thomas. You need more proof, not just your judgment. Now come on, let's get back to our planning and stop worrying, 'cause in a couple of months, we're not going to have to deal with any of these guys again. Okay?"

Thomas looked at Billy and smiled. "You're right, kid."

He sat down next to Billy, and they continued their planning. They worked until dinner was called. After hiding their supplies once more, they headed toward the mess hall.

When they entered the tent, the room was dimly lit. They each grabbed a tray as they made their way through the food line. When they reached the end, they started looking for a table. Most of the tables were already filled when Thomas and Billy noticed Drew sitting by himself.

"Are these seats taken?" Thomas asked as they walked up to Drew.

Drew quickly gathered his papers. "Only if you don't start accusing me of not letting you sit here."

"No. No more accusing. I want to apologize for what happened this morning."

Drew sat up straight. "Really?"

"Yeah."

"Thanks!"

"No problem." Thomas smiled and noticed Drew's papers. "So, what are you writing?"

Drew remembered his papers and hastily slid them under his tray. "Oh, nothing important. Just something for back home."

"Are they worried about you?"

"What? Who?" Drew sputtered nervously.

Thomas squinted. "You know, your family and friends. Do they know you were in a coma for a month?"

"Oh, yeah. Of course." Drew laughed nervously. "Yes, they know, and they're glad to hear I recovered quickly so I can carry on with my duty over here," he continued more confidently.

"Speaking of help," Thomas continued as he noticed Kelly walking in and looking around. "Did Kelly ever find you? I know he was looking for you."

"Kelly? Oh, yeah, we talked."

"Drew! There you are," Kelly sighed, throwing his hands up. "Where have you been? I've been looking everywhere for you."

Drew shot his head up from his tray with a worried look spreading across his face.

"I thought you said he found you," Thomas said, perplexed.

Kelly sat down next to Drew. "Seriously, man, where were you? I've been needing to talk to you all day."

Drew glared at Thomas, completely ignoring Kelly. "What is your deal with me?" he snapped. "You got a problem with me? Just say it. I'm not hiding anything."

Drew stood up and started for the door, then turned back around. "Apology not accepted," he scowled, and stormed out.

Thomas was staring at the door when he saw Kelly glaring at him.

"You don't know when to quit, do you?" Kelly said, then followed Drew out.

Thomas turned to Billy, who just sat there with a blank stare.

Thomas was finally cleared to return to the front, but he would be going there without Billy, who had been taken to the infirmary. Thomas was glad to see that Billy was doing better; he had been suffering from dehydration, sleep deprivation, and a huge bump on his head. A South Carolina soldier had snuck across to their side and knocked Billy over the head, rendering him unconscious. Thomas had dragged him halfway to base camp, where the doctors had taken Billy and assured Thomas that the boy would be well taken care of.

Since that time, the South had predicted every move the North intended, consistently being the first to strike. The North attempted their own surprise attacks, but the South remained one step ahead. After each attack, the South would retreat temporarily, allowing the North to regain some ground before returning with an even stronger offensive. It was plain to see that the North was on its knees. The South continued to gain control and predicted that the North would soon be defeated.

South Carolina had almost completely infiltrated the North, making it impossible to tell allies from enemies. Every day, Thomas heard his comrades pray for mercy. They could hardly bring themselves to shoot, fearing the very real risk of friendly fire.

General Hobbs called back his army, desperate to regain control. He pulled aside a group of fifteen men, including Thomas, Kelly, and Drew, to carry out a sneak attack. Hobbs knew that if he wanted control, he would have to take every chance to attack. He ordered the men to sneak through the woods, taking them behind enemy lines.

Thomas followed the group deep into the woods before turning toward the South side. They could hear the men yelling on the field as they headed for the enemy line. Each soldier on the mission held their breath and tip-toed across, praying they wouldn't be spotted.

As they approached, they stopped to search for the best place to attack. One man ahead of the rest turned to face them, raised his hand, and signaled for them to take cover behind a tree. Before they could move, a Southerner came up from behind and slit the man's throat. Then, out of nowhere, they were ambushed. Thomas ducked behind a tree before he was noticed. He couldn't understand how the enemies had known their plan when Hobbs had only just formed it.

They were being attacked from all sides. Thomas stole a glance and saw that they were surrounded two-to-one. He debated running back to the General to warn him about the ambush, but realized he might get spotted and shot. Then he remembered Hobbs' command: never leave your own men behind.

Thomas loaded his gun and cautiously poked his head around the tree to look for a target. Once he'd spotted an enemy, he aimed and fired, watching the man fall. He reloaded and aimed again, hitting another man. He shot two more before a Southern soldier spotted him and charged.

Thomas ran toward the battlefield. He was about to reach the clearing when another soldier stepped into his path, and another blocked his right side. Thomas whipped around, seeing his pursuer stop behind him. A wall of trees trapped Thomas between the three men. There was no escape.

The three soldiers shoved Thomas up against a tree, knocking the breath out of his lungs. They moved back a bit, apparently planning to toy with him before killing him. Their red and blue striped uniforms stuck in Thomas's mind: vertical stripes covered their pants and jackets, and a blue sash diagonally crossed their torsos. Their uniforms were more elaborate than his own, which consisted of plain blue fabric with bold red stripes running vertically along the legs, a narrower white stripe in the center, and the small white "NC" letters positioned over the heart.

"Any last words?" said the tallest of the three soldiers, shoving his gun into Thomas's chest and pulling it away again.

Thomas looked back and forth between the three of them, certain that all hope was lost. He held out his gun and dropped it to the ground as he fell to his knees. The tall man nodded to the soldier on his left to pick it up.

Thomas looked up at the sky and prayed one last time.

"Please," he whispered as he slowly closed his eyes, preparing himself for what was coming.

Everything had grown quiet. Thomas opened his eyes and saw the three men just standing in fear, listening. Thomas heard absolutely nothing—no shouting or cannons being fired. Everything was still.

Suddenly he felt the wind change. The sky had grown dark and was now tinged with green. The wind grew stronger, and soon his hearing was drowned out by a deafening roar. He wrapped his arms around the tree and held on with all his might as he watched a tornado twist itself down the middle of the battlefield.

Thomas pressed his head against the tree, trying to block out the screams echoing in his ear. Then he heard a loud metallic clunk right above his head. He started to scream, but his voice was drowned out by the tornado.

The wind finally died down. Thomas slowly raised his head and saw that he was now at the edge of the woods, fifty feet away from where he had been before the tornado had struck. He also saw that two of the soldiers who had surrounded him were gone. The third was lying on the ground a few feet away; it was the soldier who had grabbed Thomas's gun, which he still clutched in his hand.

Thomas crawled over to the fallen soldier and bent down to retrieve his gun, but when he tried to pull it free, the weapon resisted, jerking him back down. Only then did he notice that the soldier had been pierced through the torso by an iron rod, his stiffened fingers locked around the gun in a grip of rigor mortis.

Thomas struggled in vain to pry the gun free from the man's hand. Spotting a stick on the ground, he slid it under the man's index finger and pushed upward with all his strength. A sickening pop echoed as the finger went limp, and Thomas fought the urge to gag as he released the rest of the soldier's stiffened grip. With the gun finally in hand, he turned toward the battlefield.

Thomas suddenly stopped. For the first time, the battlefield lay clear of smoke, the tornado having sucked it away. On the far left, a small pond shimmered, surrounded by vibrant green grass—the brightest he'd seen in months, maybe years. Beyond the treetops, faint mountain ridges emerged under the bluest sky he'd ever known. Something peculiar caught his attention: there were no clouds in sight, not even after the storm. As a bird soared overhead, Thomas found himself smiling.

"This war can't kill everything," he said to himself.

He saw where the tornado's path had cut from west to east, dividing the North and South and uprooting dozens of trees. The brief silence was shattered by the sound of gunfire, and the moment of peace vanished. Thomas sprinted, undetected, back towards camp.

14

BILLY

Billy's injury had turned out to be a blessing. After treating him, the doctors had put him on bedrest, giving him plenty of time to study the maps and plan a route for his and Thomas's escape.

He laid the map out on his bed so that he could get a good look at it. He surmised that traveling from base camp to his home would take two weeks, and it would take Thomas another half a week to reach his own home. They would travel through Tennessee, Missouri, and Kansas, where Thomas would meet Billy's family. Billy smiled at the thought of seeing his mother, his sister Sarah, and his brother Jason again, but then a tight knot formed in his chest as he thought back to how he had abandoned them.

"I'm sorry, Mama," he whispered. "But don't worry, I'll be back home soon."

He finished studying the map and hid the plans underneath his mattress. He was tucking in his blanket when Thomas burst into the tent. He was out of breath and looked terrified.

"Thomas? What's wrong?" Billy said. "What are you doing back so soon?"

Thomas turned to look at him. "I need to talk to General Hobbs," he said and rushed back out, Billy hurrying after him.

Billy caught up to him, and together they entered Hobbs' tent.

General Hobbs and Colonel Nelson were bent over a desk that took up more than half the tent, leaving only a few feet to stand in front of or behind it. They were deep in thought, studying a map and a pile of papers that were spread out on the desk. In fact, as Billy looked around, he saw papers scattered everywhere, including on Hobbs' bed and nightstand; some were even pinned to the walls and taped to the windows.

The tent was crowded with the four of them in there. Nelson and Hobbs looked up from the papers and stared at Thomas and Billy as they barged into their quarters.

"Sir, I need to tell you something," Thomas began.

Hobbs stood up, his gut pushing the table outward a bit. Nelson remained as he was.

"What is this?" Hobbs demanded in his gravelly voice. "Who are you to barge into my tent? You two are not allowed in here! Why aren't you at the front? We have better things to do than entertaining privates. Now get out, before I have you two arrested!"

Billy started to turn toward the door and whispered to Thomas to follow, but he didn't move. He stood his ground and kept his eyes fixed on the Hobbs.

"Thomas!" Billy whispered again desperately.

"Sir, I just came from the front," Thomas said, ignoring Billy's pleas. "Something happened while I was there."

Hobbs still looked irritated but allowed Thomas to continue.

"Sir, a tornado just stormed right into the middle of the battlefield."

"A what?" Nelson interjected. He stood up and started worriedly twirling his pencil-thin mustache.

Thomas looked toward Nelson. "A tornado," he repeated. "It took out half our men and half of theirs."

Nelson relaxed, but he continued to twirl his mustache. "Well, that's good!"

"I don't think so, Colonel," Thomas replied. "I still saw a lot of their men. Right before the tornado hit, they had us almost completely pushed back. They ambushed our sneak attack again."

Thomas and Billy stared at their baffled expressions. Billy, too, was in shock. A tornado…he couldn't believe it. *Wow, of all the times I had to be on bed rest,* he thought.

Thomas interrupted Billy's thoughts as he continued.

"I'm not sure, but I think we should double up on security here. The enemy could be coming here to attack."

"Yes, you could be right. Do you know how many men are still out there?" Hobbs asked.

"No, sir. I came to report as soon as I could. But the tornado took out a lot of our men."

"So, we're going to need more men," Hobbs concluded. He turned to the Colonel.

"Nelson, gather up some men to inspect the field, then come back and report." Nelson saluted just before rushing out of the tent.

Hobbs then turned to Billy and Thomas. "Good work, men," he said.

He left the tent and ordered his soldiers to remain alert and prepared for anything. For the next week and a half, the men were all on guard duty around the camp to await a Southern invasion.

The next few weeks were quiet, and the General gave another announcement: if an attack were going to take place, it would have already happened. Everything went back to normal. Soldiers came and went from the front. Billy caught word that the North was slowly regaining control.

Hobbs continued to send his men to the front to help keep the South pushed back, and fewer men stayed at camp. Thomas and Billy had a few chances to continue planning, and as the days grew colder, their plan to run away would soon take place.

A few days later, Thomas and Billy ate breakfast before heading back to their bunk, where Billy saw a letter sitting on his cot. It was from his mother. He tore it open and started laughing as soon as he began to read it.

"My brother is already excited for his birthday, which is still a month away. He thinks that when he turns ten he'll become the man of the house."

He looked up to see Thomas reading his own letter, presumably from Ily. Thomas's grin was even wider than his own.

"Good news?" Billy asked Thomas, who continued to read his letter. "Thomas?" he repeated.

Thomas finally looked up.

"Huh? Oh, yeah!" he chuckled. "Ily says she's relieved to hear from me and is glad that I recovered. She was worried sick about me. But other than that, I think we finally have our names picked out. If the baby is a boy, Ily wants to name him after me, but I think I convinced her to go with Todd. And if the baby is a girl, we're going to name her Hazel."

"What's wrong with 'Jr.?'" Billy asked.

"Nothing. Just that my father's name was Thomas, so I'm a Jr. I just don't want to call my son Thomas the Third. You know what I mean?"

"Yeah. My dad wanted to name me after him, too," Billy recalled. "Would you believe I could have been Abraham the Fourth? My mom wouldn't allow it. All the first-born sons are named Abraham. Even my two uncles and my aunt all named their first sons Abraham. I would have been the fourth since I'm the oldest out of all my cousins, but my mom didn't want that. You can imagine how confusing it is at all the get-togethers now."

Thomas laughed. They spent the rest of the day writing back to their loved ones, working on their plans, and practicing drills before going to bed.

Billy couldn't tell whether it was day or night. Blood and sweat flooded his eyes as he tried to wipe them with his hands, blistered from constantly shooting at nothing. He ducked behind sandbags and noticed that something was different. He'd seen the battlefield dozens of times, but this time it seemed very different. All was calm and silent, and there was fog in the air instead of smoke. He could only see ten feet in front of him, and suddenly he spotted a man—no, a boy—staring at him. Their eyes locked, and their movements seemed to become one.

Suddenly, he recognized the boy and his chest began to sting. At the same time, he saw fear frozen on the boy's face. He seemed closer now, and Billy could see that his eyes were black voids.

Billy didn't make a sound as he hit the ground. All he heard was a single word.

"Retreat."

Billy shot up and clenched his chest. He was breathing heavily, trying to convince himself that it had only been a dream.

He looked around, wondering what time it was. It was still dark out, with a hint of light signaling that the sun would soon rise. He began to close his eyes again when a man burst into the tent, screaming,

"Get up! We're under attack! The camp is being ambushed!"

The men jumped out of their cots and rushed to retrieve their weapons, still in their long johns.

Billy put his hand on Thomas's shoulder. Drew wasn't in bed. In fact, his cot was still made up from the night before.

"Where's Drew?" Billy asked. Thomas looked back at the cot, then grabbed Billy's arm.

"Come on!" he said through gritted teeth as he pulled Billy out of the tent. They stepped outside and froze in place as they took in the scene: soldiers were running back and forth, and lieutenants were commanding left and right. The soldiers were shooting through the thickness of the trees. People were fighting all around, even over dead men.

A man came running at Billy and tackled him to the ground. Billy lost his breath as the man pinned him down with all his weight, one arm crushing his chest. He leaned his face into Billy's and bare his blackened teeth.

"So young, such a waste," he snarled as Billy choked on the man's stale, hot breath. Billy turned his head at something that flashed in his eyes—the blade of a knife held above his head.

He closed his eyes, and yet he could still see the man's face. He had one good eye that pierced into Billy's soul, while his left eye was held shut by a long scar running diagonally down his cheek. Billy realized that his nightmare had come true.

He opened his eyes to see Thomas's arm extended towards him. Billy looked beside him and saw the man who had been on top of him, now staring at him blankly with blood dribbling down his chin. Then Billy noticed blood dripping from the butt of Thomas's gun. He took Thomas's hand and slowly stood up, only to immediately bend over, coughing out the stale breath that lingered in the back of his throat.

"You okay?" Thomas asked.

"Yeah, I am now," Billy replied shakily.

By the time they'd loaded their rifles, they had become useless, for the battlefield had become too hectic for a clear shot at the enemy. So, they converted their rifles into clubs. They were walking on fallen soldiers—dead, half-dead, and even alive. Grunts and screams rang in Billy's ears.

Billy didn't know when, but somehow, he and Thomas were separated amidst the chaos. Billy started dodging left and right, struggling to stay on his feet. He tripped over a corpse and was prepared for the dead men to break his fall when he felt a tug on the back of his shirt. He was relieved that Thomas had found him again—only it wasn't Thomas.

This man was even more rugged than the first man who had pinned Billy down. He moved his hand up and yanked Billy's hair, pulling his head backward to expose his neck before pointing his rusty, blood-soaked blade under his throat. Billy reached for his own knife, which hung from his belt. As the man brought his knife closer to Billy's throat, Billy plunged his own knife into the man's overgrown gut. The man released his grip as he stumbled backward, joining the pile of corpses on the ground. Billy fell to his knees next to him and yanked out the knife. He said a prayer as the man closed his eyes.

Billy looked up and noticed Thomas being attacked in the distance. His body filled with rage as he stood up and raised his rifle to his shoulder. With one eye closed and the other staring down the barrel, he aimed in Thomas's direction, shaking from excitement. He finally had a shot at the attacker's head. He tried to steady his body to pull the trigger, but just as he did, Thomas swung around and was now in the line of fire. Billy's body froze as he heard a loud *BANG*, the bullet speeding through the air.

"Thomas!" Billy screamed, and squeezed his eyes shut. When he opened them, he saw a soldier go down, revealing Thomas standing behind him, frozen with shock. Billy breathed a great sigh of relief. He fell to his knees again, his breath slowly returning, when something caught his attention out of the corner of his eye: Drew. He was slipping into the woods, casting a suspicious glance back at the ambush before vanishing into the trees. Billy hurried after him.

Drew was unaware of Billy trailing him, but he remained cautious nevertheless, weaving through the woods with sharp twists and turns to throw off any potential followers. Luckily, though, Billy now knew this forest better than a deer would. He almost revealed himself, though, when Drew stopped suddenly in front of a big oak tree. Billy had to watch where he stepped: the sun was up now, its light shining through the treetops.

Billy hid behind a hedge and watched as Drew waited anxiously for something—or someone. He waited for a while until finally, someone came from around the big oak tree. He was tall and thin and wore a captain's uniform. Billy could see grey hair sticking out from under his military cap, matching his beard.

The two men saluted each other.

The captain spoke. "I see you received my message, Sergeant Ord."

Billy's eyes grew wide. "'Sergeant?'" he whispered to himself.

"Yes, Captain, I did", Drew replied. "As for why I am here?"

"The General is very pleased with your work thus far. If it weren't for you, North Carolina would still be in control. You have provided us all of their weak points, and now you have led us to their camp."

"Thank you, Captain. I'm just doing my duty to keep peace and do what is right for my state."

"You keep up the good work, and you might become a Lieutenant. We're glad you've recovered well from your mishap. You're too good of a man to lose."

"That was a stupid mistake that should have never happened. Those men were careless," Drew said, his temper rising.

"Maybe so. But you're lucky they found you and took you to their medical camp. You were also being careless, trying to bury that mine while you were being watched. You're lucky that you killed those soldiers first before they finished you. Does anyone else suspect anything?"

"No, sir. They all took me in as one of their own. Well…there's one private, but I can handle him."

"Are you sure?"

"Yes, sir. No one believes him. He tried convincing another, but I gained Kelly's trust the moment we met."

"Well, do what you have to before they get too far."

"Sir, yes, sir."

Two days had gone by since the ambush—and since Billy had discovered the truth about Drew. He hadn't found a chance to tell Thomas yet. Ever since the discovery in the woods, Drew had been hanging around Billy and Thomas constantly. Thomas tried to ask him why, but Drew continued to insist that he was now indebted to him and Billy for saving his life. But Billy knew the real reason—and so would Thomas if it weren't for Drew's constant presence. They hadn't even had time to continue planning their escape, and their window of opportunity was quickly closing.

Meanwhile, Billy, Thomas, and the other soldiers had been dealing with the aftermath of the bloodbath from two days prior. They had been tasked with gathering the corpses and separating their own dead from that of the South. They hauled their own men deep into the forest, dug a ditch, and threw them in, creating a graveyard. The wounded soldiers who overfilled the hospital were transported to other medical camps. The wounded from the South, however, were executed and thrown into the ditch, as well. It took a week to restore order to the camp. Tents were rebuilt, blood scrubbed out of the grass.

Once their work was finished, Colonel Nelson announced the total damage.

"After South Carolina's stunt, we've lost more men than ever. We're still tryin' to figure out how they got through our wall of men and found our camp. But we're close. I also have news from the other camps. They're not doing so bad, but they're short on men, too. We'll find out what's happening, and we'll defend our own."

He took a moment to look around.

"We ask all of you men to keep your eyes and ears open. If you hear or see anything, report it immediately."

He dismissed them, and Billy started to walk away when Drew stopped him.

"Where you goin', Billy Boy?"

"It's just Billy, and I have to use the latrine," Billy said coldly.

"Woah, sorry." Drew held up his hands and stepped back, grinning slyly.

Once Billy reached the outhouse, he glanced around to make sure no one was watching, then turned and ran to General Hobbs' tent. Sneaking through the door, he saw that Hobbs was once again accompanied by Colonel Nelson.

Billy cleared his throat to get their attention.

"You again?" Nelson scowled as Hobbs stared at Billy.

Billy chuckled a little. "Yes, it's me again." He felt a wave of bravery come over him. "Sirs, I need to have a word with you."

"We're a wee busy," Nelson said impatiently. "If ye haven't noticed, a war is goin' on, and we're losin' control. Unless ye have important information, we don't have time for yer childishness."

"Sir, I do have important information," Billy said, standing his ground. He noticed Nelson roll his eyes. "I know why we've been getting hit so hard and why every move we make, the South beats us to it."

"Ha!" Nelson scoffed. "Why, yer just a kid—an orphan. How could you possibly know?"

"We have a spy among us," Billy announced confidently, ignoring Nelson's mockery.

"Ye think there's a spy?" Nelson sneered.

"Silence, Colonel," General Hobbs said sternly. "Let the boy speak." He squinted at Billy curiously. "How do you know? What makes you think there's a spy?"

"I don't think—I know for a fact. I saw him run into the forest and I followed him. I heard him talking to a captain from the other side."

"You followed him? Son, that was dangerous—you could have been killed."

"That's not the point, sir. The captain called the soldier I followed 'Sergeant Ord.'"

"Ord? I don't think we have a Sergeant Ord."

"That's because he goes by the name of 'Private Drew.'"

The General froze. "Do you have any proof?"

Billy's eyes widened, and his heart sank to his stomach. The wave of bravery had suddenly disappeared, leaving him to fend for himself. He hadn't thought about how he would prove such a serious claim. He had to think—and fast. He glanced at Nelson, who had a smirk on his face.

"No. I don't have any proof," Billy admitted, staring at his combat boots. He heard Nelson scoff, but suddenly an idea struck him. His eyes lit up. "What if you check his cot?" he suggested. "You might find something there."

"We can't check anyone's cot if you have nothing for us to go off of," Hobbs reminded him.

"I know what I saw, though, sir."

"We can't just take yer word for it!" Nelson interjected. "It'll be yers against his."

"Colonel, I can handle this." Hobbs said. He turned back to Billy and let out a deep breath.

"Did you happen to catch the name of the captain that he was supposedly talking to?"

Billy thought for a moment. "No," he said disappointedly.

Nelson extended his arm toward Billy. "Oi! You see? For all we know, he could have been going after one of our own."

"But sirs," Billy continued, "I heard the captain tell Ord that if it weren't for him, North Carolina would still have the upper hand."

He saw both of their jaws drop.

"Well, even so," the General said, "we don't have time to go through each bunk searching for evidence we may or may not find. And besides, this Ord soldier might get spooked, and then we'll never catch him."

"What if I told you he bunks in the same tent as me?" Billy said.

"How convenient!" Nelson exclaimed. "Oi! How do we know yer not the spy and just tryin' to set some bloke up?"

Billy's eyes widened. "What? Why would I draw attention to myself if I were a spy? Which I am *not*!"

"I don't know—maybe to get us off yer track! Blimey!"

"Nelson, you're getting out of hand," Hobbs boomed. "This is Billy Jenkins. He's a good kid. I know all about him. He's here just trying to help his mother and siblings stay on their farm. Right?" he said, turning to Billy.

Billy nodded.

"He's far too young to be fighting in the first place," Nelson muttered.

Billy's eyes shot up. He darted his gaze between the two of them. What did Nelson mean by that? Did they know his real age? No, they would have sent him back home if they did—right? He tried to remain calm as his palms began to sweat.

"He's just trying his best to help out," Hobbs said. "After all, Nelson, you did tell the men to come to us if they knew anything. And that's what he's doing, isn't it?"

Billy sighed, relieved that the General was defending him.

"Yes, General Hobbs. I'm just being cautious, that's all," Nelson said bitterly.

"Right. I understand." Hobbs glanced at Nelson, then back at Billy. "Well, we'll take a look and see what we can do about an inspection. But, Billy, you do understand that for a surprise inspection, no one can know when it will take place. Understood?"

Billy stood at attention and raised his hand to the corner of his eyebrow. "Sir, yes, sir."

He stood with his hands behind his back until General Hobbs dismissed him.

Billy found Thomas, Kelly, and—unsurprisingly—Drew standing around a fire pit alongside a few other soldiers. Now that the days were growing colder, it was better to be by the pits than in the freezing tents.

Billy scooted in beside Thomas and tugged at his elbow. Thomas didn't notice until Drew spoke up.

"Thomas, I think Billy needs you."

Billy lowered his eyes and cleared his throat as Thomas turned to face him.

"Sorry, Billy. Didn't see ya. How long have you been there?"

"Not—"

"Not long—he just came up," Drew answered, interrupting him. "Feel better, Billy Boy?" He gave Billy a wink.

"Oh, well, why don't you join us and have a cup of coffee?" Thomas offered.

"Yeah, that's a good idea," Drew agreed. "Here, let me get the cup for ya."

He walked over to the coffee station and returned with a full cup. "There you are."

Billy noticed that Drew kept staring at the cup as he handed it to him. His suspicion aroused, he reached for it but let it slip through his hands. The tin cup crashed to the ground, spilling its contents.

Billy watched Drew's smile fade as he stared at the empty cup.

"Oops, I'm so clumsy. Sorry," Billy said, feigning sheepishness.

It took Drew a moment to finally look up at Billy, his face wearing a weak, fake smile.

"No problem. That coffee was stale, anyway. I'll get you another—no trouble."

He came back and offered another cup to Billy. Just as Billy was about to reach for it, a sergeant grabbed it out of Drew's hands.

"Thank you, Private. This will hit the spot."

"Ah, Sergeant, that was for Private Billy, uh—sir."

Billy watched Drew try to remain calm.

"He can get another," the sergeant said, raising the tin cup to his mouth.

Before he could take a sip, Drew knocked it out of his hands. Hot coffee splattered everywhere, and the sergeant's face turned red with rage.

"What in the Devil's war is wrong with ya?"

"Sorry, sir, but I know that stale coffee isn't fit for a fine man like yourself."

"What's your name, Private?" the sergeant demanded, his eyes blazing with anger.

Drew stood at attention with his right hand raised in a salute. "Private Drew, sir."

He remained at attention until the sergeant saluted back.

"Private, get down and give me fifty," the sergeant ordered.

Drew dropped to the ground and began his push-ups without hesitation.

Billy pulled Thomas away, figuring this would be his only chance to talk to him while Drew was occupied. They walked to their tent while Billy caught him up.

"What?" Thomas exclaimed. "How could you go to them without any proof? And the inspection? When is it?"

"I don't know. Hence, *surprise* inspection."

Thomas looked concerned, but his worry deepened when they saw General Hobbs and Colonel Nelson approaching the tent. Another sergeant by the name of Rows arrived and called out their names— Billy, Thomas, Kelly, Drew, and Marvin, the other man who shared their tent. They were being summoned for the inspection.

All five of them lined up and followed the General through the tent flaps.

"Attention!" Rows ordered.

They stood lined up by their cots with their hands behind their backs.

Rows began with Marvin's cot. He flipped over the blankets and mattress pad, then moved to the footlocker and ordered Marvin to open it. The sergeant dumped its contents onto the disheveled cot and rummaged through Marvin's clothes and letters.

"All clear, sir," Rows reported to Hobbs and Nelson before moving to Thomas's cot. He repeated the same routine and gave it the all-clear.

Next was Billy's cot. Billy stood at attention as the sergeant tore apart his bed and footlocker. He held his breath, trying to think of an excuse for the notes that were about to be discovered. At first, Rows didn't seem to notice, but then he scattered the notes all over the cot.

"What's this?" He shoved the papers in Billy's face, so close they moved with the air of his breath.

"It's a map, sir."

"I can see that. Why do you have it, soldier?"

Billy started to panic, trying not to look at Thomas in fear of incriminating his friend. *They're supposed to catch Drew, not me,* he thought anxiously. Sweat dripped down his face and chills crawled up his back. He couldn't help it—his eyes darted to Thomas and then back to Sergeant Rows. Then it hit him.

"I'm teaching my little brother about our country, sir. I can show you in my letters."

He could have shot himself for saying that, knowing there were no letters to back up his lie. He held his breath, waiting for a response.

"That won't be necessary, soldier. As you were."

Billy's arms fell to his sides as he let out a sigh of relief. His knees felt weak and stiff at the same time.

Sergeant Rows then moved on to Drew's cot, and Billy's anxiety spiked again. He wanted to tear through his things himself. Rows disassembled the cot one layer at a time, pausing just before flipping over the pad. Billy's heart sank when he saw that nothing was underneath. Rows then commanded Drew to open his footlocker. Drew moved casually and seemed unusually calm.

Rows grabbed the footlocker and dumped it out onto the floor, sifting through its contents. All he found were clothes, spare rifle parts, and a Bible. Sergeant Rows picked up the Bible, fanned through its pages, and—nothing. Nothing at all.

Billy couldn't believe it. Did Drew know?

He glanced at Drew's face and caught a fleeting smirk.

It only took Hobbs and Nelson a few days to finish the rest of the inspections. They caught some men with moonshine and drugs and punished them for it, but the wrong men were being caught. After the failed inspection, Billy knew no one would believe him anymore.

Everything Thomas had pointed out about Drew's suspicious behavior suddenly began to make sense: why he was constantly sneaking off; why he always kept an eye on Thomas and Billy, but was never around when they wanted to do the same; why he'd lied about seeing Kelly when he hadn't.

Billy would have to take matters into his own hands—but he couldn't get caught. No one could know, not even Thomas; not until he had something solid on Drew. Billy trusted Thomas, but the idea of Drew always hanging around him was unsettling.

Later that night, Billy was woken from a deep sleep by the sound of shuffling inside the tent. He slowly opened one eye and saw Drew, who stuffed some things into a bag, then glanced around the tent before slipping out the door.

Quietly, Billy climbed out of his cot, pulled on his pants, and tiptoed to the tent door. He saw Drew heading toward the woods again. He ducked down and began following him.

This time, Drew didn't travel far. The person he was meeting was already waiting for him.

"I received your message that you needed to speak with me urgently," the other man said.

Billy's eyes widened as he recognized the voice. It was the same captain that Drew had met the last time he'd followed him.

"Did something happen with those men you were concerned about?" the captain asked.

"They performed a surprise inspection," Drew replied. "I heard the General talking to Billy, the kid I told you about. It was Billy's idea for them to search. While I was on my way to clear my bunk, I saw Hobbs and Nelson walking toward our tent, so I couldn't remove anything."

"Did they find any of your notes?"

"No, just the Bible. They checked my bed last, so while everyone was watching them tear apart the first man's cot, I was able to hide my notes."

"Good."

Billy gasped loudly enough to wake the whole camp. He clamped his hand over his mouth and held his breath. Luckily, they didn't hear him.

"Now," the captain continued, "you said Billy tipped them off? I told you to do whatever it took to eliminate the problem. Did I not?"

"Yes, sir. You did, and I tried. I tried to poison his coffee, but he's such a klutz."

"Listen, Ord. We gave you this job because we knew you were good. But if you can't handle it, we'll replace you. And you know what that means for you. You'd better handle it because otherwise, you'll pay for your failure—with your life."

Drew stood at attention and saluted.

Billy ran. He ran deeper into the woods, away from the battlefield, away from camp, and away from Drew. He kept running. He wanted to run all the way home. He tripped over a dead branch and fell, rolling into a tree stump. He lay there with his eyes closed, replaying Drew's conversation with the captain.

He couldn't believe it. Drew had listened in on his conversation with the General. He knew Billy had followed him into the forest on the night of the ambush. He'd even found out about the inspection and hid his notes—Billy's evidence. Now Billy had put his own life in jeopardy, as well as Thomas's.

Billy lay there until the sun began to rise, casting silhouettes of the trees and bushes. He decided that it was time to head back to camp, but when he tried to stand, a sudden pain in his right leg forced him back down. Rolling up his pant leg, he saw that his ankle was red and swollen. A throbbing ache shot up his leg, making him wince. He rubbed his ankle carefully and was relieved to find that it wasn't broken, just badly sprained. Using a nearby tree for support, he pulled himself upright, doing his best to avoid putting weight on it.

He limped out of the woods just as the camp was starting to wake up. His mind was awake and alert. As he was heading back to the tent to find Thomas, Billy bumped into him.

"Woah, Billy, where were you?" Thomas said. "I woke up and your cot was empty."

But Billy couldn't tell him—not yet. He still needed evidence and a solid plan to expose Sergeant Drew Ord, the spy.

"Uh—I couldn't sleep," he muttered, keeping his head down.

"Nightmares again?" Thomas asked. Billy nodded, still staring at the ground.

"Woah. Hey, Drew, you having nightmares too?" Thomas teased as Drew approached them.

"What?" Drew said.

"Billy can't sleep 'cause of his nightmares," Thomas explained.

Billy glanced at Drew's cot, figuring that he had returned to put back whatever he'd stuffed into his bag the night before.

Drew shot Billy a look, then smiled as he slung his arm around Billy's neck.

"Oh, yeah, those damn dreams. Right, Billy Boy?"

"Yeah. Well, I better get dressed," Billy said tersely as he broke away from Drew's grasp and disappeared into the tent.

Thomas and Billy stood in front of the fire pit. The days were growing colder as winter crept closer. Billy scanned the men standing across from them and realized that Drew was nowhere in sight. His heart raced for a moment, but he calmed himself.

As long as I'm with Thomas, everything will be okay, he thought.

He moved closer to the fire. His hands were freezing, along with the rest of his body. The cold wind whipped against his face but he tried to ignore it. He had to stay focused on the escape plan, and how close he and Thomas were to putting it into action.

Thomas and Billy's escape had been meticulously planned and practiced repeatedly. When the time came to leave, no unexpected obstacles would stand in their way. They had memorized the tower guards' positions and shift changes, ensuring the perfect moment to move undetected. Once they made it past the guards, the rest would be smooth sailing, allowing them to quietly make their way back home.

A smile crept onto Billy's face as thoughts of his mother and siblings filled his head. He imagined wrapping his arms around them, feeling their warmth. Then he remembered the gloves that his mother and sister Sarah had knitted and sent to him. He leaned over to Thomas.

"I'll be back. I'm gonna go get my gloves. Do you want to come with me?"

"No, I'll be okay," Thomas said, ruffling Billy's hair.

Billy limped back to the tent, his ankle still sore from earlier. Just as he reached the tent flaps, Drew suddenly pushed through, nearly knocking him over.

"Excuse me," Billy said indignantly.

"No, excuse *me*," Drew sneered as he rushed off.

Something about Drew's tone made a chill run down Billy's spine. He shook the thought away and reminded himself to hurry back to Thomas, especially with Drew out there now. He grabbed his gloves and hat, and just as he was about to step outside, he stopped, slowly turned around, and stared at Drew's cot.

"I wonder…"

He peeked outside to make sure no one was watching. Ensuring that the coast was clear, he quietly hurried to Drew's cot. He knelt by the footlocker first. It looked battered, with dents on the top and sides. The words "Private Drew" were etched on the lip. He scoffed as he read it, well aware that Drew was no private.

Billy ran his hand over one of the latches and silently scolded himself as he remembered that only Drew could open it. Still, he might as well try. He pulled up the first latch, and to his surprise, it came undone. He moved to the left latch and pulled it up; it, too, came undone. His hands slid to the center, and he gently yanked the lid, but it didn't budge—it was still locked. He ran his fingers over the keyhole and let out a sigh of disappointment. Of course, it was locked. Drew was a spy, after all.

Turning toward the cot, Billy grasped the mattress and blankets and took a deep breath. *What are the chances?* he thought as he lifted the mat.

He exhaled sharply when he saw what lay underneath. He couldn't believe his eyes. Balancing the mat with one hand, he reached for the contents beneath it: some loose papers and a small black notebook with a pencil hanging from it. He opened the notebook and skimmed through the pages. His eyes widened with every turn.

Drew had everything. Every detail about North Carolina and its troops was contained in the small notebook. He had their entire schedule, from mealtimes to roll calls, wake-up and bedtimes. He had copies of their maps, routes, and positions. He had written down the names of all their weapons, including secret weapons that hadn't been released yet. There were details in that notebook that even Billy hadn't known about.

Billy gathered the rest of the papers and headed for the door, but he froze as he saw Drew entering the tent. Their eyes met and Billy's heart raced. He stuffed the papers into his coat as casually as he could and nodded to Drew, brushing past him as he headed outside.

He searched for Thomas at the fire pits, but he wasn't there. He guessed that he might have gone to the mess hall to get out of the cold, but he wasn't there, either. Just as Billy was beginning to worry, he spotted Thomas out of the corner of his eye, walking out of the latrine. He began to rush toward him, but Thomas stopped to talk to another man.

Billy was about to call out Thomas's name when he felt an arm wrap around him. A hand muffled his mouth as he was yanked behind a bush.

A voice whispered into Billy's ear. He recognized it instantly—it was Drew.

"I can't let you tell."

A sharp, burning pain shot through Billy's side, and he collapsed to the ground.

15

THOMAS

When Thomas returned to the fire pits, he noticed that Billy had yet to return. He didn't think much of it at first, but as the fire began dying out while the sun disappeared behind the trees, he grew concerned. He headed to their tent to look for him, but as he walked in, he only saw Kelly and Marvin sitting on their cots.

"Hey, have either of you seen Billy?" he asked.

They both shook their heads.

Thomas paused, thinking. "Have either of you seen Drew?" he asked, grasping at straws.

Again, they both shook their heads. Thomas began to panic.

"You okay, Tom?" Marvin asked, noticing his unease.

"I'd feel better if I found Billy. Would you mind helping me?"

"Sure," Marvin replied.

Thomas looked toward Kelly, hoping for his help, but Kelly didn't acknowledge him.

"Kelly?"

Kelly looked up, a little annoyed. "Alright, fine. But if you say one thing about Drew being part of his disappearance, I'm done helping."

By then, the sun had completely set, leaving only a faint glow peeking through the trees. It was getting harder to see. They decided to start at the fire pits and split up to search the entire camp. Thomas went to the mess hall, Marvin headed to the camp hospital, and Kelly began walking around the perimeter. By the time they regrouped, the only light came from the torches set up around the camp.

"Alright, I'll check the privy," Thomas said. "You two check our tent and the mess hall again."

"Thomas, we already checked—" Kelly started.

"I don't care. Check them again!" Thomas snapped.

Neither Kelly nor Marvin argued further, and they headed to their respective search areas.

Thomas knocked on the outhouse door.

"Billy, you in there?"

A drunken soldier stumbled out, reeking of alcohol.

"No Billys in there, only a James," the man slurred, leaning against Thomas in a stumbling salute. "At your service," he hiccupped.

"At ease, soldier," Thomas said as he pushed him off.

"Already done that, sir," the man replied, grinning wryly.

Thomas smiled awkwardly and walked away. On his way back to the tent, he heard a cough. He stopped in his tracks, turned toward a bush, and waited. Hearing nothing else, he continued toward the tent.

He met up with Marvin and Kelly, who hadn't had any luck.

"Where do you think he's gone off to?" Marvin asked.

Thomas hesitated, then spoke. "I hope he didn't follow Drew again."

Marvin looked confused.

"Thomas, I told you, if you bring Drew up, I'm done," Kelly interjected.

"What does Drew have to do with any of this?" Marvin asked.

"Shh." Thomas held up a hand.

"Excuse me? Don't shush me after I just helped you!" Marvin snapped.

"Do you hear that?" Thomas whispered, shushing him again.

Marvin's eyes widened as he clenched his fists, but before he could respond, they all heard someone yelling.

"Man down! Help! Help! Man down!"

Thomas darted toward the sound, Kelly and Marvin close behind. As they came closer, Thomas realized that the cry had come from the direction in which he'd heard the cough earlier.

A circle of men had already formed around the man in question. Thomas pushed his way forward, trying to get a better look.

"Get a doctor!" a man called out from the circle.

Three soldiers in front of Thomas turned and ran for the infirmary, leaving a gap in the crowd. Thomas stepped forward and finally saw who everyone was gathered around.

At first, he couldn't tell who was lying on the ground or what had happened to him. Then the flicker of a lamp revealed a bloodstained shirt. A glint of light shone on the victim's face, and Thomas gasped. He dropped to his knees and gently pulled the man—no, boy—onto his lap. A tear slid down his cheek as he whispered his name.

"Billy."

Billy gasped for air and weakly opened his eyes, searching for Thomas.

"Tom?" His voice was barely a whisper.

Thomas shushed him gently.

"It's going to be okay. I'm here. You don't need to talk. You're going to be okay."

Thomas looked down at Billy's wound, his face stricken with grief.

"Oh, Billy...what happened?"

Billy closed his eyes and slowly managed to speak again.

"Drew," he said faintly.

"What?" Thomas asked, leaning closer.

"You were right. I-I have notes to..."

Billy began coughing, blood flecking his chin.

"N-notes to prove that Drew is a-a spy."

He coughed again, his body trembling. He tried to move his hand toward his coat but lacked the strength.

"Thomas, in my coat...are s-some..." He took a deep, labored breath. "N-notes about D-Drew."

Thomas frantically searched Billy's coat but found nothing.

"Billy, there's nothing in your coat," he said, his voice breaking.

Billy suddenly sat upright, clutching at Thomas's chest with what little strength he had left.

"You have to find him, Thomas," Billy whispered urgently, beforing collapsing back into Thomas's lap.

"You have to...before...before..."

Billy's voice faded, his breathing shallow. He stared at Thomas with wide, desperate eyes.

"He has notes. Secrets. Things us privates don't even know. If he gives that to the South..." Billy took another rattling breath. "North Carolina is lost."

Thomas's head snapped up, scanning the crowd of men gathered around.

"Where's Private Drew?" he demanded. "We need to find him! He's the one who did this. He's dangerous. Search everywhere! In the forest, in the camp, everywhere. He needs to pay for what he's done to Billy, to us, and to North Carolina!"

Billy tugged weakly on Thomas's sleeve, whispering into his ear again.

Thomas looked back up at the crowd.

"Search the clearing in the woods! Go!"

Half the men took off in all directions, disappearing into the night.

"Thomas?" Billy's voice was faint.

"Yes?" Thomas replied, holding him close.

"Can you tell them?"

"Tell who what?" Thomas's eyes began to well with tears.

"My mother...before the army does. Can you tell her I'm sorry?"

"Don't talk like that. You're going to be alright," Thomas said, his voice trembling.

Billy shook his head weakly. "Promise me. Promise you'll make it home...to be a father. You're a great father."

Thomas's tears finally spilled over. "And you're a great son. Your father would be so proud of you. I am too."

Billy gave him a faint smile.

"Thirteen," he whispered.

"What?"

"I'm really thirteen..." he repeated, his breaths growing shallower. "I love you, Dad."

Thomas froze, the weight of Billy's words hitting him like a blow to the chest.

"I love you too, son. And I promise."

Billy exhaled one final breath, and Thomas felt his body go still.

"Billy?" Thomas shook him gently. "Billy!"

Tears streamed down his face as he hugged Billy's lifeless body tightly to his chest.

Kelly knelt down beside him.

"Thomas, I'm so sorry," he said softly. "He was a good kid. Too young. I know how you must feel. When I lost Jack, I lost a brother."

Thomas looked up, his grief replaced by anger.

"Don't," he said sharply.

"What?" Kelly was startled by the harshness in Thomas's tone.

"Don't! Don't say it. You didn't know him, so don't even try to feel sorry for him! If it hadn't been for you always sticking up for Drew, we would've already seen through him!"

Kelly stood up, stunned. He backed away, hurt and bewildered by Thomas's outburst.

Suddenly, they heard: "Make way! The doc is here! Doctor Whittle is here to help!"

Dr. Whittle hurried forward but stopped dead in his tracks. His face turned pale as he saw Thomas huddled over Billy's limp body.

"Oh...Oh no," he whispered, his voice filled with sorrow.

Thomas watched as Dr. Whittle and two other surgeons took Billy's body to the infirmary to prepare him for a proper burial. Thomas was about to follow them until he heard Drew's voice coming from the trees.

He and the rest of the men watched as Drew stumbled out of the trees. His hair was disheveled and he was out of breath. He noticed Thomas and Kelly at the front of the group.

"Thank God. Thomas, I've been looking everywhere for you. You've got to help me. Billy's dead, and they think I killed him."

Thomas glared at him, his soft brown eyes filled with rage.

Drew turned toward Kelly.

"Kelly?" Drew said his name sincerely, his dark blue eyes full of sorrow. It was almost believable. He reached his hand out to him, but Kelly backed away.

"No one will vouch for you," Thomas said. "We all know who you are and what you did."

"You don't understand," Drew pleaded. "I saw the real killer. I saw him sneak into our camp and stab Billy. When I saw Billy was dead, I tried to track his killer down."

He inched closer to Thomas.

"Tom, you have to believe me. I'm angry, just like you."

Thomas's eyes widened.

"There isn't one bit of truth in that story. Billy wasn't dead yet. You left him to die. He clung to his last breath until he could tell me everything. He told me all about your notes and secrets."

Thomas turned to his fellow soldiers.

"Billy told me that Drew knows secrets not even our Colonel knows. And how do you think Billy knew that?"

He turned back to Drew and pointed.

"With *your* notes that you hid under your cot. Billy was coming to show them to me, but before he could, you yanked him back and killed him. Didn't you?"

Drew was speechless. Thomas noticed he was sweating. "Didn't you—Sergeant Drew Ord?"

Drew's jaw dropped and his eyes widened with shock. "How—?" he began, but he was interrupted by Thomas.

"Billy followed you—a couple of times, actually. He just didn't report it because he knew no one would believe an eighteen-year-old. Especially without proof."

"Drew, is all that true?" Kelly asked in disbelief.

Drew ignored him.

"It's *your* fault he's dead," he snapped back at Thomas. "He wouldn't be dead if you hadn't filled his head with made-up stories about other people. You say he didn't have proof, and yet suddenly you believed him just because he was dying."

Thomas couldn't control his rage any longer. He knocked Drew down with one blow to the chin.

Suddenly, two officers marched out of the forest. Thomas, Kelly, and Drew—who was still lying on the ground—watched as the officers approached, lugging along a young boy in handcuffs.

"What is this? What is going on here?" General Hobbs demanded as he joined the middle of the circle.

"Sir, I believe these papers will explain everything." One of the officers reached into his overcoat and pulled out some sheets of paper and a little black notebook. He handed them to Hobbs.

The officer continued. "We chased down this traitor," he said, gesturing to the boy in handcuffs, "after he was seen talking with *him*." He pointed to Drew, who still lay on the ground. "We saw them trade papers and then flee the area."

"Is this true?" Hobbs asked Drew.

Drew remained silent.

"I also heard a soldier was wounded?" Hobbs inquired.

"You heard correctly, General." Thomas said, stepping forward. "Unfortunately, Billy didn't make it, sir."

"Billy?"

Thomas nodded his head.

"Did anyone witness the attack?" General Hobbs asked. He was starting to get frustrated.

"No, sir. But with his final breath, he told me that Sergeant Drew Ord was the one responsible for his death. He was on his way with proof that Drew is a spy. In fact, you're holding the proof in your hands right now."

"Where is Billy now?"

"Dr. Whittle took him," Thomas said.

"Good." Hobbs then turned his full attention to Drew.

"Sergeant, huh? We'll see about that. Arrest him."

The officers placed handcuffs around Drew's wrists.

"Why was he on the ground?" the General asked Thomas. Thomas rubbed his knuckles and couldn't help but smile.

Thomas and Hobbes made their way to the infirmary. Dr. Whittle uncovered Billy's body for Hobbs to see. Hobbs' face softened when he saw Billy's expressionless face.

"Billy…" he muttered to himself. "Isn't he the one who came to warn us about Drew? He even gave us the idea to perform an inspection. We didn't do a very good job of protecting him from Drew."

He turned to Thomas.

"I'm so sorry. It must be hard losing your best friend."

"He was like a son to me," Thomas said tearily.

"What I don't understand is that we searched his cot, and we didn't find anything! How did—"

Thomas cut him off.

"He tried to fool us. But sir, if it hadn't been for Billy's bravery, our side would have been defeated by now. The notes that the officers found contained information that would have put all of us in our graves."

"You're right, Private Milton. Billy Jenkins will be honored."

Thomas frowned.

"Don't fret, Thomas. Billy will have his justice. The killer and his accomplice will be hanged tomorrow morning, and we will see to it that young Private Billy receives a proper burial."

The next morning came quickly. Thomas felt like he hadn't slept in weeks. Today was the day he and Billy were supposed to head home. But Thomas knew that he couldn't go now, at least not yet. He couldn't leave until he saw Drew hanged to his death.

He was deep in thought when he heard roll being called, and he hurried to his station. As he waited to be called, he noticed two ropes hanging behind Colonel Nelson.

After roll was called, Colonel Nelson shifted his attention to Drew and his accomplice, who were being led onto the platform by the same officers who had caught them the night before. The soldiers stood at attention as the officers bound the traitors' hands behind their backs and covered their heads with burlap sacks, while the Colonel read their Charges from a piece of parchment.

"We are gathered here today to witness the death of two men: Sergeant Drew Ord and Private James O'Malley. These two men have been found guilty of espionage and treason—right here in our own camp. Therefore, under General Donald Hobbs' command, I, Colonel Drake Nelson, condemn these men to their deaths."

He turned to Drew and James.

"Any last words? Speak now, or forever hold your peace."

He waited for a response but was met with silence. Nelson nodded to the executioner, but just then, a cry was heard.

"Wait!" James screamed, his voice muffled by the burlap sack.

Nelson raised his fist, halting the execution. He walked over to James. "What do you have to say?" he asked.

"Please, sir, I didn't do anything wrong," James pleaded tearfully, his face still covered. He spoke with a heavy lisp. "I was just supposed to pick something up and take it back to my general. I didn't know what I was walking into."

"Hush up, boy!" Drew yelled suddenly. "Stay strong. We die with honor! South Carolina will honor us for keeping our mouths shut. Now hush, you dim-witted child!"

"No, sir!" James replied, choking on his tears. "I don't want to die! Not in the Army *or* with honor. I'm only ten. Please help me! I didn't even want to join, but the South made me."

"You're weak," Drew said disgustedly. "No wonder the General sent you. He was sending you to your death either way. He figured if the North caught you, they'd kill you for being a spy, and then you'd be out of his way."

James turned to Colonel Nelson. "Don't you see I had no part in this?" he asked desperately. "See, he just confessed! Please don't kill me—I'll do anything."

"How do we know you're not lying?" Colonel Nelson asked.

"Because if I were a true spy, I would've kept my mouth shut, and we'd be dead already. But I don't want to die!"

Colonel Nelson removed the boy's sack from his head. He was a young boy with a dirty face and clumps of mud that made his blond hair appear black. His face reminded Thomas of Billy's, with the same small nose.

"Please, sir," James whispered.

The Colonel saw truth in the boy's teary green eyes. He turned to one of the officers.

"Officer, untie him and take him to my quarters. I'll deal with him."

The officer untied James and hauled him away. As soon as the boy stepped down from the platform, Nelson gave the signal. James gasped, squeezing his eyes shut as Drew was hanged to his death.

"Thomas—Good, yer here," Colonel Nelson greeted as Thomas walked through the Colonel's tent. As Thomas entered, he saw James seated on a chair behind the table.

"Thomas, I wanted you here because you and Billy were close," Nelson said. "I thought you should hear this, as well."

He sat down across from the boy, while Thomas stayed standing with his arms crossed in front of his chest.

"Alright, son, yer gonna tell us everything you know," Nelson ordered.

"But sir," James said desperately, "I already told you everything. My captain told me to meet a man at a clearing in the middle of the woods. He told me that if I brought him back what I was supposed to, he would send me home." He glanced between Nelson and Thomas. "I had no part in whatever Sergeant Ord did to get hanged, or in killing one of your men. I never killed anyone."

"Did you know Drew?" Thomas asked calmly.

James began to shake his head, but then looked at the ground and nodded.

"Well, what is it, yes or no?" Colonel Nelson was growing impatient.

"Yes *and* no!" James wailed. "They wanted children so they could use us for the small jobs—digging holes, chasing the rats out, running onto the field to see if anyone was hurt. We could hide better in the trees, too. Drew gave me some tips on how to climb trees, and how to hold a rifle in case something happened. Other than that, he didn't waste his time with the boys. That's what they called us: 'the boys.'"

Colonel Nelson took a deep breath as he stood up. "Well, kid. I'm bloody well gonna send you home."

James' eyes widened. "What?"

"Yer too young to be here. War ain't puppies and rainbows for a ten-year-old." He shot a glance at Thomas. "Billy was even too young."

Thomas looked down, knowing just how young Billy had really been.

"Well, you wait here while I set up a ride to take you home," Nelson concluded.

"Thank you, sir!" Jack exclaimed tearfully.

Nelson nodded his head and left the tent, leaving James with Thomas.

"How old was Billy?" James asked.

"He was eighteen, just a kid like you."

146

"Were you close to him?"

Thomas nodded and cleared his throat. "He was like a son to me."

"I'm sorry."

A tear ran down Thomas's cheek. "It wasn't your fault."

"It's not yours either, sir."

"Yes, it was. I should have listened and kept a better eye on him."

"Naw, it was the crummy South," James said sadly.

Thomas smiled slightly. "You're a good kid," he said.

All the men at camp attended Billy's burial. They came to pay their respects to the brave young soul who had sacrificed himself for his fellow soldiers.

Thomas felt sick. Billy deserved to be laid to rest in his hometown, at an old age, in a proper coffin—not wrapped in cloth and covered haphazardly with dirt. Gripping the shovel, Thomas stepped toward the grave, scooped up a handful of dirt, and closed his eyes.

"I'm so sorry, Billy. I will keep my promise," he whispered to himself just before throwing the dirt on Billy.

General Hobbs allowed Thomas four days to grieve and recover. During that time, Thomas visited Billy every day, aware that once his break was over, he'd have to return to the frontlines.

On the fourth day, Thomas knelt next to Billy's grave and laid down some flowers, a handful of dandelions that he had found on his way to the cemetery.

"Well, Billy, this is it. Tomorrow's the day. Everything's packed and ready. Leaving you here won't be easy, especially like this, but I guess it's now or never."

He placed his hand on the loose dirt.

"I'm going to miss you, Billy. You should be coming with me—or better yet, it should have been me, not you."

A tear landed on the dirt. Thomas wiped his nose and eyes with the back of his glove.

"But don't worry, I'm going to keep my promise and tell your family first. And I'll make it back to my own family, too. I just want you to know I couldn't have done it without you, kid."

He stood up and gave Billy one final salute.

Things at the camp had finally calmed down since Drew had been executed, and North Carolina was slowly gaining control.

After his visit with Billy, Thomas spent the rest of the day reviewing his plans again and again, memorizing every step. He needed it to be just right; any mistakes could cost him his life.

He mentally reviewed the plan one last time: he would make his way to the tree, carrying only the essentials. From there, he'd head to the creek leading to the front, but instead of turning left, he'd take a right and circle back around the camp.

He had to be exceptionally careful. He would need to cross enemy lines to ensure his men wouldn't spot him, then make his way back, traveling through Tennessee, Missouri, and Kansas to deliver the news to Billy's mother. Only after that could he head home to reunite with his beautiful wife and meet his child.

Thomas smiled. He couldn't wait any longer. He wanted to be home.

The next morning, he was up before dawn, ready to put his plan into motion. He was eager to begin, but he had to be patient; he couldn't afford to raise suspicion. He stood in line for roll call, waiting to be summoned to the front, where his plans would either succeed or unravel. After roll call, he made sure to finish everything on his tray, ensuring he could save his rations for the journey ahead.

Finally, the time had come. Thomas made his way through the forest, running the plan through his mind, but he couldn't help but feel anxious.

What if I get caught by my own side? Will they believe that I got turned around? Will they point me in the right direction, or see through my lie and turn me in? What if the other side catches me sneaking around? What will they do?

These thoughts raced through his head as sweat collected on his brow. Then the image of Ily holding their baby made him forget his worries.

No! he told himself. *I'm doing this for Ily and our baby, and for Billy and his family.*

He clung to this thought as he approached the tree with the squirrel hole in which he had hidden his supplies. Working swiftly, he packed his map, a few cans of beans and crackers, and an extra blanket, just in case the weather turned. It was November, and while the snow had been light so far, it was only a matter of time: each night had been growing colder, and the air hung heavy with moisture. He also packed one extra pair of clothes, a small compact shovel, a case of bullets, a lantern, and extra matches. He swung his knapsack over his shoulder, along with his rifle. After filling his canteen at the creek, he made his turn without hesitation.

Thomas approached the first watchtower, which stood in the middle of a clearing, where the forest ahead marked the border of South Carolina. Before entering the clearing, he took note of the tower. The guards were scheduled to switch out at eleven-thirty. He sat and waited, studying the tree line for movement. Right on the dot, he saw the guard at the top of the tower disappear, and Thomas dashed towards the other side.

He didn't stop running until he was deep in the woods. He looked back and saw nothing but trees. He took a short break, just long enough to look at his map and compass. Suddenly, he heard a twig snap. He dodged behind a tree just as he heard voices coming his way.

"Over here!" a raspy voice called out to another man. "I saw an intruder run into our woods."

"Are you sure?" replied the other man in a softer, high-pitched tone.

"Of course. You reckon I be lyin'?" the first man snapped back. Thomas could tell he had a temper. "No one comes into these woods an' gets out alive while *I'm* on watch duty."

Thomas held his breath.

"I'll catch whoever dared step into this here forest," the ill-tempered man continued. "An' I guarantee they won't be stepping out again—or anywhere else, for that matter. You can bet yer children on it."

"I-I don't have any children," replied his stuttering companion.

"What?"

"Children. I don't…"

"Aw, hush yer tongue!"

Thomas heard their footsteps slowly fade away. He waited a while before stepping out from behind the tree, then began to backtrack, staying close to the tree line.

As he pressed on, Thomas did his best to move silently, aware that the two men might still be tracking him. Every sound put him on edge. A quick glance at the map showed that he was nearing a point parallel to his camp. Despite being surrounded by South Carolina's dense trees, he didn't dare let his guard down. He longed to reach Tennessee, where he would finally feel free and safe.

The snap of another branch jerked Thomas back into reality. He spun around but found no one there, which only heightened his anxiety. Then he realized that the sound had come from somewhere above his head. He was about to look up when he felt a great weight collapse onto him, forcing him to the ground.

"Foun' yous!" a raspy voice called out. Thomas recognized it instantly. As he gasped for air, he locked eyes with the man's steely gray gaze and summoned all his strength to push him off.

"I do love me a challenge," the man said, his scruffy face twisting into a sneer. As he struggled, Thomas's gaze fell on a long scar that started on the man's chin and snaked its way down his throat.

Thomas reached for his rifle just as the man knocked it out of his reach. He was an ogre compared to Thomas.

"Come on, soldier," he said to Thomas tauntingly. "You gotta be more creative than that to beat me."

Just then, another pair of arms reached around Thomas, knocking out what little air was left in his lungs.

"Fine work, Terry!" said the man with the scar.

"Th-thank you, Elroy," his friend stammered.

"Now, *this* here is creative!" Elroy said with a wry grin as he pulled a knife from his belt. Thomas tried to pull free, but Terry tightened his grasp. For a petite man, he was surprisingly strong.

"You know something…Thomas?" Elroy said, yanking Thomas's dog tags and reading them before tossing them to Terry. "I tell all my victims the story about my scar. That way, I know the last thing they think about: me!"

He rubbed his hand along the scar.

"It's more like a beauty mark to me. Am I angry that I got it? Yes, but not at myself—at you Northern soldiers. You and your side did this to me. I was scopin' these woods to make sure they were clean of y'all varmints. I didn't watch my step and landed right on a landmine. When I woke up, I noticed I couldn't feel my face. As I raised my hand to touch it, I felt something sharp and pulled it out—and now I have this here scar to remind me to watch my step and kill any Northern soldier who ever dares to get past me. And, Thomas, I always catch 'em."

He stood before Thomas with his knife in hand.

"Now, prepare to pay."

Just as Elroy lunged at him, Thomas sashayed to the left, the knife nearly nicking his ear. Then he heard a pained grunt. He felt Terry suddenly release his tight grip as his body went limp and collapsed onto the ground, still holding Thomas's dog tags.

Thomas's eyes widened as he looked down and saw the knife stuck in Terry's heart. He and Elroy froze in shock as they realized what had happened.

Elroy turned towards Thomas, shaking with rage.

"You! Cuss in all tarnation, you made me kill one of my own men. He was my friend. You're gonna pay!"

He lunged forward once more but missed yet again as Thomas jumped to the side.

"That makes us even, then," Thomas said bravely. "Because one of your men also killed a close friend of mine. He was like a son to me."

"I don't care about yer son. And we're not even, either. You probably killed the man who done it, anyway."

"Yes, we did—because he was a spy."

Elroy gasped. "No! Drew!" He looked up from the ground, angrier than before. "Cuss in all tarnation! Now that's two friends yer gonna have to pay for!"

He charged at Thomas, this time knocking him to the ground. Thomas gasped for air as Elroy looked down at him, holding his knife under his throat.

"You're a lost soldier now," he said menacingly.

BANG!

Elroy's eyes shot wide open as he moved his hand to discover a hole in his chest. He looked back at Thomas before collapsing onto him, pinning him down. Thomas grunted as he pushed him off, still gripping the pistol he'd managed to steal from Elroy's belt.

Thomas rose to his feet, catching his breath. As he took a step forward, he felt a sharp, throbbing pain and looked down to see Elroy's knife plunged into his abdomen. He toppled to the ground, and the world faded to black. Then his eyes fluttered open, and he saw only Ily.

She was sitting in her chair in their living room, dressed all in black. She stared blankly across the room at an open casket. Then she stood up, carefully cradling their baby as she walked over to the casket, where Thomas's body lay. She placed the stillborn in Thomas's arms and looked down at them one last time.

"Our prayers were not answered," she murmured as she slowly closed the casket.

16

ILY

"Ily?"

Eddie was confused to see Ily standing on his and Betsy's porch in the middle of the night. As he came closer, he could just make out her face in the darkness and saw that she had been crying.

"Ily, what happened?" he asked. He helped her inside and guided her to the sofa.

"I'm sorry it's so late. It was just so horrible." Ily could barely speak.

"Who is it, Eddie?" Betsy said, coming out of the bedroom. "Ily! Are you okay?" she said, sounding surprised.

"I'm sorry to wake you, but I had to talk to someone," Ily said earnestly.

"Is everything alright?"

Ily shook her head nervously. "No, it's...it's Thomas." She let out a loud sob. "I just know something is wrong now. I've had the worst nightmare ever."

"It couldn't have been that bad," Eddie said nervously.

Ily shot her head up and stared at him.

"I shut the lid to Thomas's casket with our baby in it." She broke down again.

Betsy rushed to her side.

"Oh!" She wrapped her arms around Ily and pulled her into a tight hug, her motherly instincts kicking in. "There, there, it's all over now. It's going to be alright."

"Yeah, I'm sure Thomas is just fine," Eddie reassured her. "You've started getting letters from him again, haven't you?"

Ily thought for a moment, then froze as she realized that the letters had stopped again.

"I think the last letter I got was in September! One was about him waking up from a coma after stepping on a landmine. And another was about a spy among them." She gasped. "What if he's stepped on another one and doesn't wake up this time? Or the spy got to him?"

"September? Eddie, it's November." Betsy was worried now.

"Now, girls, you two are working yourselves up," Eddie said. "This is Thomas we're talking about. Thomas Milton. The man who could raise a barn all by himself."

He stared at Ily, whose head was still buried in her hands.

"Ily." He knelt down and took her hands. Her eyes were red and swollen. "Who was the one who helped everyone replant their crops after the first dust storm buried them?"

"Thomas," Ily answered weakly.

"That's right. And who was the one who helped rebuild the Joneses' house after another terrible storm?"

"Thomas did," Ily answered again.

"Thomas did!" Eddie repeated. "See? If Thomas could survive dust storms, he can survive a bullet."

"What?" Ily gasped.

Eddie realized what he had said.

"Not that he did get shot!" he said. "I was just trying to say that Thomas could survive anything life throws at him. Plus, he knows he can't die, because if he did, you would kill him."

"Edward!" Betsy scolded.

"It's okay," Ily said. "Eddie helped me remember how strong Thomas is. When Thomas gets something in his head, he doesn't quit 'til he's tried his hardest. And if that doesn't work, he tries even harder. He's strong-willed and will stop at nothing till he gets to where he wants to be."

"Exactly," Betsy said. "And another thing, Ily: it's already been three months. If something had happened, you would've known by now."

"I just can't help but feel…" Ily began.

"You're just feeling this way 'cause you're almost due," Eddie said. "Plus, Thanksgiving is coming up, and you insist on cooking the turkey, even though I told you I'd be more than happy to do it. And I know you're trying to get your house clean because you also insist on hosting Thanksgiving at your place, when, again, you don't need to trouble yourself." He took a deep breath. "Whew! See? You even got me all worked up now."

Both Ily and Betsy giggled.

"What you need is a good night's rest," he concluded. He took Ily's hand and helped her up, Betsy following along. "Now, why don't you and Betsy take the bed, and I'll take the floor?"

He pushed them through the bedroom door and gently closed it behind them before they could protest..

Ily spent the next few days preparing for Thanksgiving. She would take care of everything, except for killing the turkey. She had finally conceded the job to Eddie, for which she was thankful. She knew she wouldn't have been able to kill it, especially after her nightmare.

She sat in her chair, rubbing her eight-month-pregnant belly and waiting for her guests—Eddie, Betsy, and their children—to arrive. She knew that celebrating Thanksgiving here would help to keep her from worrying about Thomas. She wondered where he would be on Thanksgiving, and if he'd even get to eat any turkey.

She smiled as she thought about the last Thanksgiving that they had all celebrated together. Thomas and Eddie would always go hunting for a turkey before the meal. Eddie would kill the turkey, claiming that it always tasted better fresh. He would tease Thomas, saying that he could never kill anything even if it was standing right in front of him. When it was time to eat, Thomas and Eddie would sit at opposite ends of the dinner table, while Ily and Betsy sat across from each other and the children sat at a smaller table. Thomas always carved the turkey while Betsy told her children to settle down. Eddie would say grace, and Ily would start building everyone's plates. This year, Ily made all the side dishes herself; she knew Betsy would be busy with Carl, but she was more than happy to do it.

Ily was deep in thought when she heard a knock at the door. She glanced at the clock.

"One o'clock, right on time!"

She took one more look at the tables that she had set up right outside the kitchen. They were set with her best tablecloths and dishes. She inhaled the aroma of the pies in the oven and all the food that had been delicately placed on the main table, where she, Eddie, and Betsy would sit. The smaller table for the children sat between the sofa and the main table. She lit two candles before opening the door.

"Hello, everyone! Happy Thanksgiving! Please come in."

Betsy, Eddie, and their children all gave Ily a hug as they entered her house.

"Mmm, something smells wonderful, Ily!" Eddie complimented as he walked in carrying the turkey.

Ily smiled.

"Thank you. Your turkey looks wonderful too! The pumpkin and apple pies are still baking, but they should be done by the time we're ready to eat them. That way, for dessert, we can have warm pie with homemade ice cream!"

The children cheered.

"Ily, you've outdone yourself," Betsy marveled as she gave Ily a one-armed hug, holding her sleeping six-month-old baby boy in her other arm. "Look, even the table is set with candles. Ily, we could have helped you."

Ily beamed. "I know, but it really was no trouble. It kept me busy, and I was done before I knew it. Our crib is up if you'd like to put Carl in there while he sleeps."

Betsy smiled as she took Carl into the nursery.

"Looks great, Ily!" Eddie added, giving Ily a kiss on the cheek.

"You can set the turkey right here," Ily pointed as she guided him to an empty spot in the middle of the table. "Did you have to go far to catch it this year?"

"Nah. I didn't catch one this year. I got a really good deal from Mr. Kay. He told me he had an extra one that he didn't need, so he offered it to me. I took him up on it because I knew it'd be different this year, since I couldn't make fun of Thomas for being such a sissy."

Their laughter was brief and awkward. Eddie cleared his throat.

"No, actually, I was going to let Noah tag along this year and let him catch it, but we didn't have time to go."

"Oh! Well, I'm sure this one will be just as good," Ily said.

"Dad?" Noah said to Eddie.

"Yes, Noah?"

"May I sit at the adult table? I ain't a kid no more."

"Of course you may!" Ily answered on Eddie's behalf. "It'll be nice to have a new face at the table."

They all sat down and held hands to say grace. Eddie looked up toward Noah.

"Noah, how 'bout you say grace?"

Noah glanced up.

"Me?"

"Why not? You're not a kid anymore. Go ahead."

Noah cleared his throat excitedly. Just as he was about to begin, there was a knock at the door.

They all stared at the door. Another knock came and Ily stood up to answer it. She wondered who it could be; her guests had all arrived. She knew there was no mail, and she wasn't expecting anyone else.

"Yes?" Ily asked as she opened the door to a worn-out middle-aged man. Tufts of gray hair stuck out from underneath his hat. Ily noticed a medal pinned above his heart. She recognized the military insignia and began to feel weak in the knees.

"Good afternoon, ma'am."

The man tipped his hat and peered inside, seeing that Ily had guests.

"Er, any of y'all Ily Milton, wife of Thomas Milton?" Ily noticed that he spoke with a Southern accent, and she began to tremble.

"Yes, I am Ily. Is everything alright? Is Thomas alright?" She tried her best to stay calm.

He removed his hat, exposing a whole head of gray hair. "Ma'am, my name is Mr. Robertson and I am with the North Carolina military."

Ily lost her breath and found herself in the arms of Eddie, who had overheard the conversation and rushed to her side.

"I am very sorry to inform you that your husband, Private Thomas Milton, was…killed in action."

Ily went limp again in Eddie's arms. Betsy jumped up from the table to help her to her chair.

"Oh, Ily!" Betsy exclaimed.

Ily stared blankly at the floor.

"I—I can't believe it…Thomas…gone…forever."

She looked up and saw Mr. Robertson still standing by the door.

"How? When?" she asked, her voice breaking.

Mr. Robertson looked out toward his car and then at his watch. He was in a hurry—he had more families to visit, more bad news to deliver—but he knew he couldn't leave her in the dark.

"Please, sir, put my mind at ease," Ily whispered. "I need to know."

Mr. Robertson paused before sitting down. Ily caught him looking at her stomach and started to rub it.

"It's our first," she said.

"What?" He blinked away from her stomach.

"Thomas was excited about becoming a father. He would have been great at it." Ily's smile faded. "How was he found? Are they sure it's him?"

"We'll give you two some privacy," Betsy said as she pushed Eddie toward the tables.

"Please sit." Ily patted the chair. "This chair has been empty for eight months; it's Thomas's chair." She brushed a tear from her eye.

"I can sit on your sofa," Mr. Robertson offered.

"No, please, it's been empty for too long. Please sit," Ily insisted.

Mr. Robertson handed her an envelope as he sat in the chair. Ily read the front of the envelope, which was addressed to her.

"I remember the day he was summoned to boot camp. It all started with a letter." Ily sighed as she wiped another tear, meeting Mr. Robertson's eyes. "And now it ends with a letter. How was he found?"

"A couple of our men noticed he was missing, so they gathered a group to look for him and saw a body lying near the border by one of our lookout towers. When they turned the body over, they saw Thomas's tags."

Ily began to sob again. Betsy and Eddie rushed back to her side, and Betsy placed her hand on Ily's shoulder.

"I'm sorry," Mr. Robertson said. "He fit all of Thomas's descriptions. It looks as though he saw a Southerner trying to cross and successfully stopped him. But his own life was also taken by someone who snuck up behind him when he was trying to head back to safety. There isn't any other explanation. No one can figure out why he would be around that area in the first place. The guards that were on duty in the tower nearby said they never saw anything. General Hobbs knew Thomas was a good man. He died trying to do the right thing."

"Why were they surprised to find him where they did?" Eddie asked.

Mr. Robertson cast a glance toward Eddie. "Well, where Thomas was, no soldier had any reason to be, nor were they ever stationed there. He was heading in the exact opposite direction of the battlefield. The only plausible explanation is that he saw a Southerner trying to cross into our territory. But even then, we still don't understand how Thomas could have encountered this soldier."

"What are you trying to say? Eddie asked. "That Thomas was trying to run away? That doesn't sound like our Thomas! Was he a guard in the tower?"

"He could have been assigned as one, but he never had been before. It's possible, but we don't keep track of who's guarding—just whoever goes to the front. At any rate, the North Carolina Military would like to honor Private Thomas Milton by awarding him this medal of bravery, for not only trying to stop a Southerner from crossing to our side, but also for discovering a spy among our men. If it hadn't been for Thomas and Private Billy Jenkins, North Carolina would be at a loss right now. So, I now present this medal of bravery to you, Ily Milton, wife of Private Thomas Milton."

Mr. Robertson rose to his feet, saluted, and handed Ily Thomas's dog tags along with a small box. Ily placed the box on her lap and opened it. Inside was a medal featuring an eagle clutching a star, with small green gems at each point. A blue ribbon was attached to the star, completing the display.

"We would also like to present Private Thomas with a Purple Heart," said Mr. Robertson, handing Ily a second box.

"Wait," Eddie said suddenly. "Did you say Billy? Billy Jenkins? The boy who hung around Thomas all the time?"

"Yes, sir," replied Mr. Robertson. "Because of that spy, we lost another good man."

"Wait, Billy's dead too?"

Mr. Robertson removed his hat. "Yes, sir. Billy knew all of the spy's secrets, and the spy killed Billy for it. But luckily, Billy told Thomas just in time, and Thomas exposed the spy to the whole camp."

"Man, he was only eighteen," Eddie said quietly. "Just a kid."

"Actually, according to his mother, he was thirteen."

"What?" Eddie was shocked. "He looked way older."

"Turns out he wasn't even registered."

"Then why was he in the group with us?"

"He was just fishing and fell in. When he was saved, the men thought he had joined, and I guess he just went with it."

"Why, that sly dog", Eddie marveled. "Did he even live in Douglas, Kansas, with his mother and siblings?"

"Yes. His father died two years ago, and Billy ran away to help with the family farm. So I'm guessing he wanted to join but knew he wasn't old enough, so he tried his way and it worked."

"How'd his father die?"

"Eddie!" Betsy scolded him.

"What? Billy told us already. I just want to make sure he was telling the truth. He already lied about his age. I want to see what else he lied about."

"In a storm. Got trampled while trying to save their barn and cows." Mr. Robertson paused. "How did you know him?"

Eddie stood at attention and saluted. "Private Eddie Ryeson, sir. I'm one of the men who saved that boy from drowning that day."

"At ease, soldier. Private, huh? How'd you get released?"

Eddie lowered his hand. "My youngest passed away due to dust pneumonia. From Black Sunday."

"I'm sorry for your loss."

"She was six," Betsy said mournfully.

"Poor youngin'." Mr. Robertson glanced at his pocket watch. "Well, I best get going if I want to make it back home before the holiday ends."

He tipped his hat as he opened the door.

"I'm sorry again. Didn't want to ruin your holiday with such awful news. You have my deepest condolences."

He was almost out the door when Ily stopped him.

"What about his body?"

Mr. Robertson looked down at his feet, regretting what he was about to tell her.

"I'm sorry. I wish there was some way we could send him home, but there are no funds to relocate bodies. There are just too many to send back, and some men aren't even recognizable enough for us to know where to send them. I'm sorry."

"I'd recognize my Thomas anywhere," Ily insisted. "Did he have any pain?"

"He went quickly, if that's what you mean."

"Oh…as long as he didn't suffer," Ily said quietly.

"No, they say chest wounds can kill instantly."

Ily, Eddie, and Betsy gasped in shock.

"Oh, I'm sorry. I wasn't…I'd better go before I make things worse."

"Wait. Was he shot?" Ily asked.

"I'm not…" Mr Robertson huffed and shook his head. "I'm not allowed to say…but I've already gotten this far. It wasn't a bullet that killed Thomas, but a knife wound to the chest. Now I really have to go. I have a couple more stops to make. It was nice meeting you. I'm sorry it wasn't on a happier occasion. Enjoy your Thanksgiving meal. God bless."

He raced out the door before any more questions could be asked.

Ily stood staring at the door, speechless. Betsy nudged Eddie and gestured toward Ily with her eyes, urging him to do something. Eddie moved in front of her and wrapped his arms around her. Ily fell into his arms and broke down, bawling into his pale blue flannel shirt.

Two weeks later, Betsy and Eddie held a gathering in the one-room schoolhouse to mourn Thomas's death. The desks had been pushed together for people to set food on, and flowers were placed all over the room. Ms. Dowers, the school's only teacher, had drawn flowers around the words "Sorry for your loss" on the chalkboard.

Ily wore a long black dress with lace sleeves. Betsy had helped Ily make it, as Ily couldn't hold the needle steady enough through all her tears.

Nearly everyone in town came to offer their condolences to Ily, assuring her that if she needed anything, they were there to help. Ily was quiet through the whole night. She felt that if she even said one word, she would burst into tears.

"How are you feeling?" Dr. Rogers asked as he hugged Ily.

She shook her head as tears formed.

"Not so good, Dr. Rogers."

"Save the 'Dr.' for the office. Tonight, I'm just Almanzo, a caring friend." He gave her a wink. "I know it can be hard, but you have to stay strong for your baby."

Ily nodded. "I'm trying, Almanzo. It's hard without Thomas."

"You have a strong will. You'll figure it out. Thomas has been gone for ten months now, and you've done pretty well thus far."

"Yes, but that's when I thought that someday he'd be back, and now... now he won't be."

"You and your child are going to make it through this. You are strong, and your child is strong—just like Thomas. Stop by anytime."

"I will."

"Hello, Almanzo." Alice said, squeezing her way between him and Ily. She was wearing a tiny black dress that stopped just at her knees, with a black ruffled cape wrapping around her shoulders. "Fancy running into you here."

"I'm trying to be a good friend to Ily, who's just lost her husband," Dr. Rogers said through gritted teeth. "Something you wouldn't know anything about," he added under his breath.

"What was that?" Alice said.

"I just asked where Russel was."

"Oh, he's around here somewhere, showing off our baby. He's a proud papa!"

"Uh...baby?"

"You didn't notice I got my figure back?" she said with a twirl. "While we were in Oklahoma City getting married—oh, my God, Ily, just look at this ring." Alice shoved her hand in front of Ily's face. "Isn't it just to die for?"

Ily's eyes widened as she saw the enormous square diamond in the center of the ring, surrounded by smaller round diamonds that glittered with every movement of Alice's hand.

"Oh, I'm sorry, darling," Alice giggled. "Poor choice of words."

"Alice!" Dr. Rogers exclaimed.

"What? I said sorry. So anyway, the day after we got married, I went into labor and—Oh! Russel, over here, baby!"

Russel waved to Alice and made his way through the crowd. He was wearing a black button-up shirt with khaki pants and boots caked with dirt.

"Sorry, I was just showing off my son!" he said excitedly.

Alice took their baby and held him up for them to see.

"Russy Jr.," she giggled as Russel put his burly arm around her. "After his daddy. What do you think of him?"

Ily leaned in to get a better look at the baby, taking in every detail of his features. His big brown eyes stared back at her. Thick black hair framed his tiny face. A tiny nose sat perfectly in the center of his face, contrasting against his wide mouth and prominent chin.

Ily looked at Alice and Russel, then back at the baby.

"Well, he has your dark eyes, Alice."

"And your big mouth," Dr. Rogers added.

Alice gave him a stern look.

"Well, we better get this little guy home so we can get him to beddy-bye!" she shrilled.

She grabbed Ily's hand before turning to leave.

"I'm sorry for your loss. I don't know how you're going to raise your child all by yourself. It's just so much easier when there's two."

"Excuse me?"

"Well, now that Thomas is gone, it's just going to be you."

"Excuse me! My husband died helping other people—but I am *not* alone. Look at all these people who have come to help me grieve."

She extended her arms out toward the crowd, who was now silent.

"Everyone except for you two has told me that they're willing to help in any way they can. I'm grateful for them! And my husband is not dead. He lives on in *here*." Ily pounded her chest with her fist. "He lives on in all these people."

"Well!" Alice scoffed. She looked at the crowd in shock before storming out the door.

The crowd's silence broke as they erupted in cheer and applause.

"About time someone put that girl in her place!" one woman shouted.

Ily was proud that she had stood up for herself—and for Thomas. The townspeople continued to congratulate her as the wake came to an end.

When Ily returned home that night, she stayed up, lost in thought. She began to feel lonelier than ever before. The house felt different now, its emptiness almost tangible. As she sat staring at the wall, rubbing her stomach, she realized that it felt hollow too.

"It's okay," she reassured the baby, as well as herself. "Daddy is gone, but he is still with us. I will always be here for you, baby. Just give me a sign you're okay. I love you." Tears began to roll down her cheeks. "Please," she whispered.

Suddenly, Ily's breathing became shallow, and her body began to cramp up. She doubled over in pain and screamed. She held her stomach as the pain grew all around the baby.

"You're okay, baby. I'm okay," she panted.

The pain seemed to slow for a moment, then started up again, even more intense this time. Ily screamed in fright as she fell out of her chair onto the floor. Her hair clung to her face as she began to sweat.

"Please be okay, little one," she cried out loud.

The pain stopped again. She sat on the floor for a while before she tried to stand up, using the chair for support. The pain returned, making her drop to her knees once more.

"What is happening?" she began to cry as the pain worsened.

She rushed to her bedroom to lie down and fell asleep.

The next day, Ily felt a little better. She pulled her truck up to Dr. Rogers' office just as he was stepping out. He was wearing a brown vest with a long-sleeve shirt underneath. He pulled out his pocket watch as he noticed Ily and greeted her. He helped Ily out of the truck, making sure she didn't trip on her winter coat or slip on the icy ground.

"Hello, Ily. Good morning."

Ily greeted him back with a weak smile.

"Are you feeling okay?"

"No, not really. I'm really worried. I haven't felt my baby move, and last night when I got home, I had this sharp pain. And I'm really nauseous," she explained as they walked out of the cold and into the exam room.

"Not feeling the baby at this point in your pregnancy is normal," Dr. Rogers said as he placed his stethoscope on Ily's stomach. After a short while, he looked up, pleased. "Strong heartbeat. You say you feel nauseous?"

Ily's eyes began to tear up.

"Are you okay?" Dr. Rogers repeated.

"I just don't feel like myself. Either I have no appetite, or I eat all day. I lost my whole world. I can't sleep or eat, and I know I need to for my baby, but I just can't. I'm all alone in that house, and I just sit and do nothing."

"Ily, it's completely normal to feel this way after losing a loved one. Have you thought about staying with someone?"

"The only people I could stay with are Betsy and Eddie," Ily said. "But they have all six of their kids to think about, and I don't want to burden them any more than I already have."

Dr. Rogers thought for a minute. "What if you stayed with me tonight?"

Ily's eyes shot up.

"Oh, I couldn't."

"Why not? It'd be no trouble."

"Dr. Rogers! How could I? I just lost my husband, and you're divorced. What would everyone think?"

"Who cares what people will say? If it really bothers you, we'll tell them that you don't feel good and I want to keep you under observation. It's just for one night, or until you feel better. It's completely up to you."

Ily thought for a moment.

"Well, it would be nice not to be alone, and to be with someone who doesn't have kids," she admitted. Then she gasped, realizing what she had said. "I'm sorry. I didn't mean anything by that."

The doctor smiled. "I'll see you at seven."

Dr. Rogers held the back door to his sunroom open as Ily stepped out, then helped her to one of the wicker chairs. Despite the winter chill and the falling snow, the room was comfortably warm. Windows covered the wall, and Ily looked out as the sun set beyond the horizon. She thought about how pleasant it would be to sit and watch the sun rise and set every day.

"Dinner was delicious," she said.

"Well, thank you," said Dr. Rogers. "My mother taught me how to cook when I was twelve. I told her that if the doctor business didn't pan out, I was going to become a chef. Plus, Alice was never a great cook, so I always did the cooking."

Ily chuckled at his comment.

"I've never had steak as tender as I did tonight," she said. "Thomas would always leave it on too long."

Dr. Rogers noticed her frown and cleared his throat.

"Well, I hope your little one liked it too."

Ily frowned again.

"What's wrong?"

"The baby."

"What? Is it coming?" Dr. Rogers asked anxiously.

"No, no, it's not that."

"Oh, good." He let out a sigh of relief, but then noticed that Ily had begun to tear up. "Then what is it?"

"I'm afraid," Ily whispered. "The other night, I had this terrible pain that made me fall to my knees and cry out loud. I haven't felt the baby move at all since then."

"Being so close to your due date, it's going to be normal not to feel your baby move. It's because it's gotten big and doesn't have a lot of room to move around now."

"I just hope the baby is okay," Ily said. "I know I haven't been taking care of myself since losing Thomas. I just don't know how I'm going to do it without him."

Dr. Rogers took Ily's hand in his.

"You'll do great. I see you with Betsy's kids all the time, and you do well with them, don't you?"

Ily stared at the floor as Dr. Rogers stood up, walked to the other room, and returned with his stethoscope. He bent down next to her, placed the scope on her stomach, and listened intensely, trying to find a heartbeat. He moved the scope around desperately, and after several attempts, he looked up at Ily sorrowfully.

Ily let out a gasp and started bawling, sliding out of her chair and onto the floor. Dr. Rogers wrapped his arms around her and rocked her back and forth.

"I'm here for you," he whispered, as tears formed in his eyes.

The following morning, Ily woke up and slowly made her way downstairs. The staircase divided the main floor into four separate rooms arranged in a circular layout. To one side, a library with French doors stood invitingly, while on the other, a pink sitting room caught her attention; she suspected Alice had chosen the color. She also noticed a door along the wall leading to Dr. Rogers' office.

Ily entered the dining room, where she and Dr. Rogers had enjoyed a lovely evening the night before. To her left stood a gourmet kitchen, and another door led to the bright sunroom.

Ily turned into the kitchen where she found Almanzo sitting at the counter.

"Well, good afternoon, Ily."

"Afternoon?" Ily asked, shocked.

"It's a little past noon," he answered, looking at his gold pocket watch.

"I slept past noon?"

"Well, after being so upset last night, you needed all the sleep you could get. And I figured if my chicken Wanda didn't wake you up this morning, you wouldn't hear me, either."

He smiled as he stood up.

"I hate to leave in such a rush, but I really have to go check on a patient. Nothing too serious, just a head cold. But take your time and stay as long as you need to. If you get hungry, you can have anything you find. I shouldn't be too long. But if you don't mind, I would like to check on your baby again before you decide to go back home. It could have been the way you were sitting last night that I wasn't able to hear the heartbeat."

Ily smiled. "Of course. I'll wait for you. Thank you."

With that, Dr. Rogers was gone.

Ily sat down and took in the sight of the gourmet kitchen. Counters lined the walls, and an island stood in the center. Cupboards stretched above the counters, stopping at a window above the sink. Two tall pantry closets flanked the counters, extending from floor to ceiling. The stove and oven were built into the island, while the icebox stood along the same wall as the kitchen door. Sunlight poured in through the window, filling the room with warmth and brightness. Ily noted how impeccably clean and organized it all was.

As she continued to look around, she saw bags of flour and sugar and some apples sitting on a counter pushed up against the wall. A thought crossed her mind: she could surprise Dr. Rogers with an apple pie as a gesture of gratitude. It would also serve as a welcome distraction from everything else on her mind.

Ily prepared the crust by mixing flour and water, rolling it out, and fitting it into a pie pan, saving a bit to use as the top layer. After partially baking the crust, she worked on the pie filling, then carefully poured it in and placed the remaining crust over the top. She made a few slits in the dough before sliding it into the oven. While the pie baked, she whipped up some dumplings with country gravy—a favorite meal from her childhood and one she'd used to enjoy making for Thomas, who had loved them just as much.

"Whoo-ee! Something smells good," Ily heard Dr. Rogers say as he entered. "Boy, my kitchen has never smelled this good."

"Thank you!" Ily beamed as she set the apple pie down on the counter.

"Ooh, Is that apple pie?" Dr. Rogers said.

"Yes. I hope you don't mind."

"Mind? Heck, only if it's for me."

"Oh, it's all for you," Ily chuckled. "Just something to show how much I appreciate what you're doing for me."

"Aw, think nothing of it. I would do it for any of my patients. But now I'm glad I did it for you."

He walked up to the pie to smell it, almost burying his head in it.

"I do love apple pie. Oh!" His eyes caught a glimpse of the frying pan. "Are those dumplings in gravy?"

Ily nodded her head and couldn't help but smile.

"I made enough for both of us, if you'd care for some."

"I didn't eat much earlier," Dr. Rogers admitted, "so I would love some."

Ily set down two plates and sat beside him at the counter. She waited for him to take the first bite.

"Yum! Ms. Ily, you are going to spoil me. I may never let you leave now. At least not before you teach me how to make these," he said as he took another bite.

After their fill of dumplings and pie, Dr. Rogers led Ily into his office to check on her baby one more time. He tried again to find a heartbeat but still had no luck.

"What do we do?" Ily asked desperately.

"Well, seeing that you're due in a couple of weeks, we'll just have to wait until your body tells you it's time."

He offered to drive Ily home, but Ily politely declined, telling him he had done so much already.

As she pulled her truck up to her house, Ily sat deep in thought. She didn't want to be by herself, and yet she wanted to be alone. She began to cry, feeling lost and confused. Finally, she decided to go to Betsy's house for some company and advice.

As soon as Betsy opened the door, Ily collapsed into her arms, bawling. Betsy and Eddie guided her to their sofa.

"Oh, Betsy, what am I going to do?" Ily said breathlessly; she could barely get a full sentence out.

Betsy laid Ily's head down on her shoulder.

"Shhh, it's alright. You're okay now, darling. I got you."

Betsy sat on the sofa beside Ily, while Eddie sat across from them in a chair. The children were still in school for the next hour, and Carl was taking a nap.

"Can you tell me what happened?" Betsy asked gently.

Ily was starting to calm down a little. She took a deep breath. "Dr. Rogers can't find a heartbeat, and I can't feel the baby, and…I'm just so afraid that I've lost the baby as well as my husband."

Betsy and Eddie were shocked.

"Ily, we're so sorry," Betsy said quietly. "Are you sure you've lost the baby? What did Dr. Rogers say?" she asked as she rubbed Ily's back.

"He thinks depression could have caused it. He said that even though you might not feel depressed, deep down your body can just feel lost," Ily said with a defeated shrug. "And I miss Thomas so much that I haven't been eating or sleeping very well. Well, except for today.

I made some dumplings and gravy for Dr. Rogers, and I didn't even get sad while I was making it."

"You made Dr. Rogers lunch?" Betsy asked.

"He told me to stay with him last night so he could keep an eye on me in case anything changed. He was worried that he couldn't hear the baby's heartbeat. He kept me company, and he helped me not to think of…"

She fell into Betsy's arms once more.

"I've lost my whole family," she sobbed.

"No, you haven't," Eddie said. "You still got us."

Betsy shot him a look of annoyance.

"She didn't mean it like that," Betsy said, turning back toward Ily. "You could have stayed with us last night if you didn't want to be alone."

"I know," Ily said. "I just know you two already have enough on your plate with the kids."

"Well, yes, I suppose that's true," Betsy admitted. "They were really testing our patience last night. They knew that today would be their last day of school for a couple of days, and none of them wanted to go to bed."

"Wait—Betsy, that's exactly what she needs!" Eddie said suddenly.

"What is?" Betsy asked.

"She needs a night with her family," Eddie explained excitedly. "What do you say, Ily? We can make some hot cocoa, sing Christmas carols, trim the tree, and play games!"

"But Christmas is still two weeks away. Don't you guys trim the tree the day before?" Ily asked, not wanting to impose.

"Heck, so we have the tree up for a couple of extra days. The kids would love it," said Eddie.

"Well, it does sound like fun," Ily said sheepishly.

"Great," Eddie and Betsy said together.

As soon as the children returned from school, the house began to buzz with excitement. Eddie took the children to pick the perfect tree to decorate, while Betsy and Ily began other preparations.

"I bet they'll be ready for some hot cocoa after being out in the snow!" Betsy said.

She and Ily giggled, and Betsy was happy to see her best friend smile for the first time in a while. Having lost Carol, Betsy could feel Ily's pain, but she couldn't imagine losing Eddie. She pushed the thought away and continued helping with dinner.

When Eddie and the children returned with the perfect tree, it was 6:30, and the sky had become pitch black. The temperature had dropped below zero and the wind had picked up, bringing snow. Eddie set up the tree between the sofa and dining room table, while the children changed into their pajamas.

As they prepared to sit at the table, they all took a moment to admire the festive decorations. Each bedroom door displayed unique paper cutouts of Santa Claus, teddy bears, gifts, snowflakes, and candy canes. Streamers draped from the ceiling rafters, and the glow of candlelight illuminated the room. Betsy's finest china and tableware were set out, with a steaming roasted chicken as the centerpiece, surrounded by potatoes, yams, corn on the cob, and freshly baked bread rolls. The enticing aroma of the meal filled every corner of the house.

Eddie opened the meal by saying grace, thanking the Lord for the dinner and the people who were there to enjoy it. As soon as the prayer ended, they began piling food onto their plates and scarfing it down, silently savoring every bite until their plates were completely empty.

After dinner, they all cleaned up and headed over to the living room to look at the tree. The children grabbed more paper streamers, popcorn strings, and ornaments, taking turns finding empty branches to fill.

Ily stepped back to admire the joyful scene as Eddie playfully adorned his children with streamers and decorations. She laughed so hard that she nearly ran out of breath. In that brief moment, all her worries faded away—until she suddenly felt her knees grow wet.

For a split second, Ily thought she might have laughed so hard that she'd had an accident. But then a strong kick from inside her stomach made her gasp. She bent forward in surprise, clutching her belly. She caught her breath and carefully stood up straight when she felt another kick and doubled over again.

The twins, Carrie and Joan, noticed Ily's pain and ran to their mother.

"Mommy, Mommy," they said in unison, tugging on Betsy's dress. "What's wrong with Auntie Ily?"

Betsy looked in Ily's direction and saw her leaning up against the wall, her face red and sweaty.

"You know, baby girls, I think we wore Aunt Ily out. She needs to rest a bit."

The twins nodded their heads, shrugged their shoulders, and ran off to play again. Betsy chuckled but then looked back toward Ily. Her smile disappeared as she realized that Ily had collapsed onto the wooden floor. Betsy gasped and screamed Eddie's name as she ran over to Ily.

Eddie was sitting on the sofa between Charles and Mary when he heard Betsy scream. He shot up from his seat and saw Ily on her knees, clutching her stomach. He rushed over to her.

Ily grabbed onto Eddie and Betsy's arms and screamed as she looked back and forth between them.

"The baby. I feel...the baby," she panted.

Betsy looked at Eddie worriedly.

"We need Dr. Rogers," she said to Eddie.

Just then, their front door flew open, the wind blowing snow through the door and revealing a figure covered in frost.

"What the heck?"

Eddie and his family watched as the figure struggled to shut the door against the wind and snow. Eddie and Noah hurried over to help; it took them three attempts before they finally were able to get it shut. As soon as they did, Eddie took hold of Noah, who in turn grabbed his younger siblings. They all stood in silence until the intruder revealed themself. Eddie held his breath, ready to act if needed, as he watched the stranger remove his top layers.

"Whew. Am I glad to see you guys," the man said.

They all let out a sigh of relief as they realized that the person who had tumbled through the door was Dr. Rogers.

"You gave us a fright," Eddie said. "What the heck are you doing out in a storm like this, anyhow?"

"I was on my way to check on Ily, but this blizzard came out of nowhere, and I lost my way. Then I saw lights in the distance, so I headed toward them. Boy, am I glad I did. Who knows where I could've ended up? It was tough, though. The snow has already piled up so high. I had to walk most of the way here; there was no way I could've gotten my car through this. And that wind just kept pushing me in all different directions. A couple of times, I almost lost your lights. I sure hope no one else is traveling in this storm."

"I'm glad you found us, too," Betsy said as she walked over and stood next to Eddie.

"Yeah, but I should get back out. I need to go check on Ily. I have to tell her something."

"Almanzo?" Ily called out weakly.

Dr. Rogers caught sight of Ily, who was still laying on the floor.

"Ily!" he exclaimed, rushing to her side. His eyes filled with worry at the sight of her weak smile.

"Almanzo, the baby. I felt the baby kick."

He gave her a perplexed look.

"Are you sure?"

"Yes, pretty sure. Then, right after the kick, I became wet," she said shyly, looking with discomfort at her dress.

Dr. Rogers looked at her sorrowfully.

"Ily, I don't think…"

She cut him off. "Almanzo…I feel it coming."

"Well, then, my dear, you're about to deliver your baby."

"What?" Ily exclaimed. "Now?"

"My dear, the baby is coming whether you're ready or not," Dr. Rogers said. "I'm going to take the wind pushing me as a sign," he chuckled.

"Can we try to move her into our bedroom so she can have some privacy?" Betsy asked.

"That's a great idea. Eddie, will you help?"

Eddie nodded his head and knelt down, wrapping Ily's arm around his neck while Dr. Rogers did the same with her other arm. They gently lifted her up but quickly sat her back down as she screamed in pain.

"Ah, I think it'll be best if we don't move her," Dr. Rogers said.

Betsy turned toward Noah.

"Noah, I want you to take Charles and the twins into our room with Carl."

Noah nodded and guided his siblings to the room, closing the door behind them.

Betsy then turned to Mary.

"Mary, go and gather all the towels and blankets you can find."

Mary turned and rushed to gather them. When she returned, she helped her mother place the blankets and towels around Ily's legs.

"Thank you. Now go on with your siblings and keep them in our room."

As soon as Mary closed the door, Ily shrieked in pain.

"Alright, it's time," Dr. Rogers said.

He took his place at Ily's feet and glanced at Betsy and Eddie, who stood on either side of Ily. He then looked at Ily.

"Are you ready? Because the baby is coming, and I can already see the head."

Ily squeezed Betsy's and Eddie's hands, sweat collecting on her forehead as Dr. Rogers told her to push. She used all her strength to push back against the wall, grunting and screaming. She kept pushing until she finally heard Dr. Rogers say, "He's out."

"What?"

"Yup, it's a boy!"

Dr. Rogers held him up for them to see—a baby boy with brown hair, round eyes, and a little nose. "A beautiful, healthy boy."

Betsy took the baby to be cleaned up.

Ily turned to Dr. Rogers.

"What did you need to tell me?" she asked him.

Almanzo gazed into her eyes lovingly. *Ily,* he wanted to say, *the other night was the best night of my life, and I don't want to go another night without you.*

Betsy returned and handed the baby to Ily. Ily gently cradled the baby in her arms, kissing his smooth head.

"He looks just like his daddy," she announced with a tearful smile.

Eddie opened the bedroom door, and the children rushed out to see Ily. Joan and Carrie went to her together.

"You got a quiet baby," Joan said. "When Carl was born, you could hear him from across the world."

"What are you going to name him?" Carrie asked.

Ily looked around the room, then down at her baby boy.

"After his daddy."

Once again, the front door flew open, and another stranger stumbled through the doorway.

"What is going on?" Eddie shouted, but grew quiet as they all stared at the stranger stepping into the light.

Ily lost her breath as she said his name.

"Thomas!"

The room fell silent, except for a cry from Ily's arms.

AUTHOR BIO

Ashley Whitney is a writer, artist, and photographer based in Lincoln, Nebraska, where she lives with her loving husband and family. With a deep passion for creativity, Ashley has turned many of her dreams into reality. She designs her own greeting cards and her motto is "Everyone deserves a card," reflecting her belief in spreading joy through heartfelt messages.

In addition to her artistic pursuits, Ashley works as a preschool photographer for Lifetouch, capturing cherished smiles at daycare picture days. She has pursued her interests in photography, improv, screenwriting, and art by attending classes at her local community college. To support her creative ambitions, she also takes on other roles, including working as a DoorDash driver and assisting at a small car dealership.

A devoted follower of Jesus, Ashley finds fulfillment in her faith, family, and friendships. She's an adoring aunt to nine nieces and nephews, cherishing every moment spent spoiling them before sending them home. In her free time, Ashley enjoys musicals, plays, and Halloween festivities—including her memorable stint as a clown at a haunted attraction. One of Ashley's unique traits is that she has epiplaphobia, which is a fear of antiques. Despite this quirky challenge, she embraces life with a caring spirit and determination to pursue her goals. Becoming a writer has been her lifelong dream since elementary school, and she's thrilled to see it finally coming true. Ashley looks forward to continuing her creative journey, embracing each new chapter with enthusiasm and heart.

www.ingramcontent.com/pod-product-compliance
Lightning Source LLC
Chambersburg PA
CBHW070025260626
47159CB00005B/1959